ATTENTION, READER!

This is an uncorrected galley proof. It is not a finished book and is not intended to look like one.

Errors in spelling, page length, format, etc. will be corrected when the book is published several months from now.

This early bound edition was prepared so that you can read—months before actual publication—what Bantam Doubleday Dell and the author will be publishing.

Pg's 7 (botom)

WANDER

"I loved this book. It is so wise about love and death and the human spirit. A fine achievement."
—*Karen Cushman*

He just appears one day—a grayish dog with white-tipped ears and a tail that wags like crazy. And he keeps coming back, until it feels to James and his younger sister, Sary, as if the old stray is their very own. Soon they've given the dog a name, and after that both children are bound to protect him against all odds. Even if it means keeping him a secret from Dad.

Home has been a lonely place since Mom died last winter. Dad spends too much time apart from James and Sary, and though their aunt Lorrie does her best to add cheer, a painful silence fills their house. But now a frisky companion has become part of their lives, and if James and Sary can figure out a way to bring the dog into the family, maybe joy and comfort will tag along with him.

Readers will never forget *Wander.* Moving and gentle, this story of loss and of love's power to heal will grab hold of heart and mind.

008–012

WANDER

WANDER

SUSAN HART LINDQUIST

DELACORTE PRESS

Published by
Delacorte Press
Bantam Doubleday Dell Publishing Group, Inc.
1540 Broadway
New York, New York 10036

Library of Congress Cataloging-in-Publication Data
Lindquist, Susan Hart.
   Wander / Susan Hart Lindquist.
     p.   cm.
   Summary: Grieving for their dead mother, twelve-year-old James and his
younger sister Sary find healing in their affection for a stray dog.
   ISBN 0-385-32563-0
   [1. Dogs—Fiction. 2. Mother and child—Fiction. 3. Death—
Fiction. 4. Grief—Fiction.] I. Title.
PZ7.L6593Wan 1998
[Fic]—dc21   98-10037
                                               CIP
                                             AC

The text of this book is set in 13-point New Baskerville.

Book design by Trish P. Watts

Manufactured in (tk)

November 1998

10 9 8 7 6 5 4 3 2 1

Printer ID TK

for Debbie
always loved
always remembered
and
for her daughter Molly
who has kept us all
from wandering

CHAPTER 1

ad's leaning against the side of the pickup, just watching the hills turn color way off in the distance. He's finished mending Navarro's fence, and I can tell he's tired by the patches of sweat spreading in dark circles on his shirt. Meaning to help, I grab the shovel and start for the back of the truck, but he barely nods, his mind somewhere far off from me.

He raises his hand to shade his eyes. Slowly he steps toward the fence and says, sort of whispery, "Well, now. I wonder what the heck that could be."

The tone in his voice scares Sary and she scoots out from where she's been playing under the truck, hustling over to stand by me the way a lamb runs to its mama—except I'm not her mama, of course, just a brother five years older. But that's no matter to Sary. These days I'm what she runs to all the same.

She taps my arm. "What's that, James?" she asks, pointing to something across the field.

It takes a minute, but now I think I'm making out what they're seeing. It's a dog, way over by the timberline, just standing there, stiff as a stump, and watching us.

Sary takes hold of my hand and squeezes it hard as Dad slowly reaches for the shovel—a precaution in case the dog starts coming after us.

"James," he says. "Sary-Girl. Stay behind." His voice is calm but I can hear worry in it as clear as anything.

"What is it?" Sary whispers, tugging on my sleeve. "What is it, James? Is it a wolf?"

Just like Sary to go thinking so dramatic. "No," I tell her. "I'm sure wolves don't wag their tails when they see people."

But I'm also sure no self-respecting sheep rancher would own a dog like the one across the field from us. It doesn't look the least like any working dog I've ever seen—too tall, narrow in the shoulders, and not black and white, but grayish, almost dusty, and thin. It's easy to see why Sary mistook it for a wolf.

It keeps its distance, though, and Dad lets out a

tired sigh and lowers the shovel. "Can't say I've ever seen a mongrel quite like that. Have you kids ever seen it before?"

"Not me," I tell him.

"Me neither," says Sary.

The dog looks friendly enough, not mean or rabid, wagging its tail so crazy like that, and I'm about ready to approach it when our cranky old neighbor, Wes Tiegland, comes barreling up the road in his shiny new Dodge pickup.

Wes Tiegland's what my aunt Lorrie calls "an unsympathetic man." He blares his horn like always, and doesn't slow or even take the trouble to raise up his hand and wave. Matter of fact, he hardly makes the caution not to knock us off the side of the road. When I turn around to look for that stray again, it's hightailing it like a scared jackrabbit, making a beeline back into the woods.

Dad's expression goes grim. "Well, that's that. We're finished here. Let's go home. Lorrie will have dinner waiting."

"But what about that dog?" Sary asks. She's standing like a post with her eyes glued to the place where the stray got swallowed up by the trees.

"I'll ask around in town. Maybe Billy will know if anyone's missing a dog. He might even want to come get it."

Sure enough, Billy Nightingale would be the one to ask. He'll take in any stray. He keeps a whole pack of them out at his place at the dump off Route 5. They're always following at his heels like a bunch of little kids, yapping and nipping each other, or sleeping in the sun by some left-out washing machine or rusted car. Billy says they're not his, though, only borrowed—there to keep him company for as long as they like, but not pets to scratch behind the ears. His first words to Dad after "Hi there!" are usually "Need a dog, Mr. Christie?"

Dad always says we need a dog about as much as we need taxes.

The sun's found a cloud to hide behind and a chill's creeping up. I zip my jacket before I help Dad lift the heavy roll of hog wire into the back of the truck.

All afternoon I've tried to make myself useful. Dad's been pleasant enough, but he's kept a ways off, not saying much more than "Fetch me a handful of staples, James" or "Sary, you doing okay?"

It's not that Dad doesn't like our company. I'm sure he wants us with him, only never too close anymore—just sort of *there*, like trees, or like sky he doesn't have to talk to or acknowledge. So we load the truck in silence, the same way we do most things together now, with only a deep quiet bubbling up between us like sour water from an old ground well.

With a rusty clang, Dad latches the tailgate, then walks around and opens the cab door. "Hurry on, Sary. Climb in there with James. Lorrie will worry if we're not home soon."

"I can't find Tulip-Virginia," Sary calls out from beneath the truck. She's lying on her belly in the gravel with only her skinny little legs poking out.

Sary's got her own ideas about things. Aunt Lorrie says it's the way of being nearly seven that makes her ask questions all the time and be so stubborn. I know we'll have to carry her away screaming before she'll leave Tulip behind. She has other dolls, but Tulip's her favorite and she totes her all over the place like an extra arm or foot. I'm forever telling her she's too old to need a doll for company, but she never listens much to me.

When I climb into the truck I spot Tulip wedged in between Dad's toolbox and the shovel—her brown yarn hair mussed, her face smiling up at me with those pink sewn-on lips twisted in that silly sideways grin. I believe she had a dress when Mom gave her to Sary, but now she's only wearing layers of grime from being loved so hard.

"She's in here, Sary." I reach for the doll, then wave it over my head. "If you need Tulip so bad, you ought to keep better track of her."

My sister scrambles onto the bumper and hoists herself over the tailgate. She grabs Tulip and plops down next to me.

"And put your sweater on," I remind her. "It'll be cold back here."

For a change, Sary does as I say, then snuggles against the bale of hay with her doll. Dad gets in, revs the engine, and pulls out onto the road while I settle back to watch the long, lonely strip of asphalt stretch out in a line behind us. Mountains way off on one side. Desert way off on the other. This narrow strip of road just out in the middle somewhere. Sort of like me and Sary, I suppose, with Mom way off in Heaven and Dad way off from us.

I start to wonder about that stray. It must belong to someone. Must go someplace to sleep at night. Sary's thinking about it too; she starts babbling and asking questions like she does when her mind fills up.

"Do you think that dog's lost?" she asks, facing away from me toward the mountains. "I bet it is. Do you think it's hungry, James? And cold?" She tucks the cuffs of her sweater over her hands. "Why didn't it come closer?"

As usual, I answer as if I really know, just to keep her from asking more questions.

"It was afraid," I say.

"But it was watching us, wasn't it, James?"

"Yes," I tell her, leaning back against the hay bale and knitting my fingers behind my head.

Sary twirls Tulip's hair around her thumb and starts to hum, soft, the way she does sometimes.

I'm never quite sure what's on her mind when she hums. She gets a sort of half-smile on her mouth and a faraway look in her eyes. I like to imagine she's thinking of Mom, but once when I thought for sure she was, she turned to me right out of the blue and said, "I like chocolate ice cream best, don't you?"

I do know that Sary's humming puts Mom on *my* mind. Though I can't clearly remember, I'm sure Mom must have hummed just that way and gotten that half-smiling, faraway look in her eyes. I'm vexed I can't remember, vexed it's been less than a year and I can't even remember that much about my mother.

I stare up into the sky, concentrate on a small gray cloud, and pretend what I always pretend on my way home—from school, a friend's, from any- where. I pretend that it's Mom, not Dad's sister, Lorrie, waiting at the house for us.

The truck hits a gravel patch and we slow

7

around the big bend where Route 5 jogs before it crosses Devlin's Creek.

"Hey James! Look!" Sary's gripping my arm. "There it is again!"

I lean past her, but all I can make out is a cluster of crows in the grass.

"There's nothing," I say.

"See? Way over there by the woods."

"It's just crows, Sary."

"No, James!" She's almost frantic. "See? That stray's following us."

Sary's right. I see it now, off in the distance, where the trees hug the edge of the pasture—that old stray, trotting along in the shadows.

It seems to be heading our way, and I'm ready to knock on the roof of the cab to tell Dad to slow down, but then we swing left off the highway, losing sight of the dog as we cross the bridge over Devlin's Creek and head up toward the house.

CHAPTER 2

We take the rutted gravel road up to Lorrie's house, driving by the old garbage pit where she dug up a treasure of antique bottles last spring, and by the broken water pump with its parts all rusted together. There's wreckage from the past strewn all around the place. Like most houses this far outside town, Lorrie's is about a hundred years old and not worth much to most folks, what with its rickety barn, its outbuildings full of spiders, and its fences that topple in winter when it rains.

Everyone in the family knows Dad never intended to keep us here this long—it was only supposed to be a month or two, till we got back on our feet. But it's been almost a year since he quit his job and we moved out from town. We're accustomed to this place, Sary and I, though Dad's still restless, like an old dog that can't seem to find a comfortable place to lie down. He skips off to town to do God knows what whenever he gets stir-crazy, which is almost every night.

Sary worries that, like Mom, some night he just won't come back. But it'd be way different with him. If Dad didn't come back it'd be because he didn't want to. Not like Mom. She didn't have a choice.

When we pull up, the house is dark, but a light's shining from the little window at the back of Lorrie's pottery shed behind the barn.

Dad stops the truck by the yard gate and gets out. "Run tell Lorrie we're home, James. And ask her if she's fed Heidi."

Every morning my aunt leaves the house at dawn to stick herself away in her workshop, and she stays there all day, happily spinning wet globs of clay around and around on her potter's wheel.

Lorrie looks up when I open the door, dripping blue glaze from her paintbrush.

"Well, at last! I waited, and waited, but I had this set of bowls that still needed glazing. Everything all right? I got a little worried. Tell me that lousy truck didn't break down."

It's hard to imagine Lorrie really worrying

about the truck, or even about us for that matter. She's always as calm and steady as wood.

"The truck's fine," I say. The fence just took longer than Dad planned. He wanted me to ask if you fed the horse."

"Sure, I fed her. And as soon as I get this cleaned up, I'll feed you." Lorrie sticks her paintbrush in a jar of water and wipes her hands on the tail of her shirt. "Blue," she says. "Always blue. Don't the folks around here know there's a whole rainbow of colors out there? Why do they always want blue?" She shakes her head and grins at me. Her cupboards are full of dishes she's made that nobody will buy because they're too wild and colorful. "I know," Lorrie continues. "You don't have to tell me. A new color would be too exciting for those plain folks in town." She laughs. "I bet you're starved. Let's go up to the house."

Sary's waiting for me on the front porch, her foot stuck up high in the air.

"Pull it off for me, James," she calls, wagging her foot at me. "The boot's too tight. Pull it off."

I come up the walk and step in front of her. "You should learn to do this for yourself," I scold, tugging on her boot. You'd think she'd know she's way too old to need me for a nursemaid all the time.

Inside, Dad's standing across the room from us in his stocking feet, leaning against the wall. He nods "hi" to Lorrie. "You have paint on your nose, Little Sister," he says.

"I finished an order today. Twelve soup bowls. Plain blue, of course. For Isabelle's cousin . . ."

Dad ignores her, and I wish hard, *Please, oh please, Lorrie, don't go on.* But she does.

"I wanted to touch them up with a splash of yellow or green, but Isabelle said . . ."

Dad pulls out a chair and sits down. He'll need to change the subject now—I can feel "Isabelle" hanging in the air like a ghost.

"We spotted a stray dog up on Aaron Navarro's place this afternoon," he says.

Lorrie sighs and joins us at the table, tolerating Dad's need to steer the conversation away from Isabelle like he always does when her name comes up.

"A lost dog?" she says. "I hope it wasn't a coyote after Aaron's sheep."

"No. It was too big for a coyote."

"Did it look sick?"

"No. Seemed healthy," Dad says. "Hungry maybe, but not rabid if that's what you mean."

"Are you certain it wasn't one of Aaron's dogs?"

"Yes. It was a stray by the look of it."

Lorrie frowns. "And not long for this world, I

imagine, with men like Wes Tiegland around," she says.

Sary's eyes lock on mine. Both of us know Mr. Tiegland loves guns. And we both know he can't abide any dogs that aren't his own.

"Speaking of Tiegland," Dad says, "he drove by when we were out there, but he was so busy leaning on his horn I doubt he noticed the dog."

Lorrie's face goes cold with loathing. "Lucky for the dog. That Tiegland fellow is a pain and misery. An unsympathetic man like that would as soon kill a stray as blink at one. Just ask Billy."

Dad sets down his fork to look hard at Lorrie. "When Wes shot that dog of Billy's last year, he was just protecting his livestock. Some things can't be helped."

I remember the commotion of bad feelings that grew up between those two men after Wes shot one of Billy's strays. Even though Billy Nightingale says the dogs he keeps don't belong to him, he sure was upset when Wes came after that one, saying it was killing his sheep, and shooting it dead without as much as an "I'm sorry" to Billy.

"Who'd let a dog run loose way out here in sheep country, anyhow?" Dad asks.

"Can't imagine," Lorrie says.

"I'll ask around at Yolanda's. Strange-looking

creature, but I suppose it has to belong to somebody."

"*Who* does it have to belong to?" Sary asks.

I shake my head. "He doesn't know," I tell her. "That's why he's going to ask around, to find out who lost it."

Sary puts down her glass of milk and glares at me. "Well, how did it get lost?"

"How should I know? How does anything get lost?"

Lorrie smiles. "That sort of thing happens sometimes, Sary. The dog probably just wandered off."

Dad and I go back to eating, but I can tell Sary's itching to know more. She's fiddling with her spoon and wiggling on her chair like she's got to go to the bathroom. At last she can't stand it and turns to Lorrie, asking sort of quiet and low so she won't sound foolish, "What's wandering, Lorrie? Is it like running away?"

Lorrie smiles at her again. "No, Sary. I'd say wandering is more like taking a walk and forgetting."

"Forgetting where you belong?"

"Yes. And forgetting who loves you," she says.

Dad's finished eating. He pushes away from the table, stands up, and slips his jacket off the back of his chair.

"Don't mind if I take a ride into town, do you? I

told Ben I'd help him put up some shelves in his garage."

It's like most other nights. We've become so accustomed to Dad's leaving, he might as well ask the air, or the walls, or the floor. Lorrie's no more about to object to his going than I am, when it's clear he doesn't want to be here with us.

"Go ahead," Lorrie says as she gets up to usher him toward the door. "We'll be fine."

I can't speak for Sary, but she looks pretty resigned to Dad's going too, hardly looking up as he closes the door. She must have something on her mind, because when Lorrie leaves the room to clear the dishes, Sary comes over to stand by my chair.

"What's wrong?" I ask. She's standing with her face right up in front of mine, waiting for kitchen noises to begin so Lorrie won't hear.

She leans real close to my ear. "What if he forgets, James?"

"Forgets what?"

"What if Daddy wanders?"

There's deep worry in her eyes, but I don't have an answer for her. I reach out and take her hand.

"It's bedtime, Sary."

"When will he come back?"

"Later. Like he always does. After you're asleep."

That's what I go on telling myself every night anyway, so that's what I tell her.

"And what will he bring us?" she asks.

"Something," I say, knowing that even though Dad will leave again in the morning before we come down for breakfast, there will be a stick of gum or a jawbreaker from the machine at Yoland's Cafe waiting on the table for each of us. And when we go outside, we'll find our boots lined up and waiting by the porch door, freshly cleaned.

CHAPTER 3

Most days breakfast comes and goes without Lorrie, since she's usually in her workshop by the time Sary and I come downstairs. But Saturday is Lorrie's day for housework, and she's made pancakes for us.

I'd like to stay here all morning, eating and lazing. But that would never sit well with Lorrie, so I finish fast, rinse my plate, and head for the door.

Sary swipes her sleeve over her milk-covered lips. "Where are you going, James?"

I glance at her, then at Lorrie. "Out. I've got chores."

Lorrie always says she doesn't know much about child-rearing, but that hasn't stopped her from knowing about chores. I think she likely read somewhere that chores build character, because right from the start, she went at them like a religion. According to her, kids need them, and that's all there is to it. At least kids my age. Seems all Sary has to be accountable for is putting the cap on the toothpaste and picking up her room. I'm the one stuck with jobs like hauling garbage and mucking Heidi's stall. Today's not so bad, though—just watering Lorrie's garden.

Sary retrieves Tulip from beside the syrup bottle, slides out of her chair, and crosses the room to me.

There's no use fighting it. Sary will follow me no matter if I want her to or not. That's just the way it is now, Sary and that doll tagging after me wherever I go. It's not her fault I'm the only one around for her to play with since we moved from town—and sometimes, just sometimes, I'm even grateful for her company.

"Bring your jacket," I say. "There's a wind."

Lorrie agrees, calling out from the laundry room. "That's right. And I'll be going to town for groceries in a while. So listen to your brother, Sary."

Sary sticks so close to my heels she's nearly stepping on me all the way around the house to the back garden. I haul the hose across the yard to the flower bed while she stands a ways off, gazing up at the thin streaks of white floating across the sky.

"It's going to rain," she says.

"No, it isn't. Move aside, Sary." I yank the hose. "You're standing on it. I've got work to do."

I pull the hose over to the camellias and lay it on the ground. Overhead, the sun's sliding in and out from behind the clouds. The idea of rain coming makes watering the flowers seem like wasted time, but I'm duty bound to keep Lorrie's plants alive.

Lorrie's made a big point of teaching us that. The yard is ringed with all kinds of crazily painted pots she's made, and in every single one she's started something growing. Lorrie likes to collect sprigs off plants, then poke them into fresh patches of dirt, or into one of those antique bottles she keeps filled with water on the windowsill over the kitchen sink. She says only good can come from trying to green up the earth, even in such a small way.

I move on with the hose. A spray of drops hits the azalea bush.

"Water from the bottom," Sary nags. I glare at her, trying to will her to mind her own business. But she smiles up at me as innocent as apple pie and I let the spray drop to the base of the plant. She looks away from me, staring into space and humming.

I finish with the azaleas and start heading across the grass to turn off the water. But a flash of movement in the woods at the far end of our pasture catches my eye.

I stop by the fence and signal for Sary to be quiet. She tiptoes to me slowly.

"What?" she whispers.

I motion toward the woods. "Did you see that?"

The sun rolls out from behind one of those lacy clouds and spreads a patch of light over the grass. I squint hard, pointing to a place just beyond the far pasture fence.

"There! There! See? It's—"

"That dog!" Sary says, drawing Tulip close to her.

I warn her to keep still. It sees us now, but it stays still too, watching us from half in, half out of the shadows.

"Let's go after it," Sary whispers.

We glance at each other. Words like "vicious" and "rabies" occur to me, but without another word we leave the garden.

Sary gets afraid and tugs on my jacket.

"You sure we ought to?"

I shush her. "Go back to the house if you're too scared."

We take it slow to keep from spooking the dog. Sary's peering around me to check on it every step or two. She stays so close this time, she really *does* tread on my shoes. We're almost to the end of the pasture when the dog gets skitty and turns around to run back into the woods.

We stop at the fence to watch it go.

A tall row of old cottonwood trees used to stand by this fence—used to, until one stormy day last winter when Dad got into a fury and cut them down, one after the other. I watched from the upstairs window, fear-struck and crying as he took the chain saw and just cut them off at the bottom and let them fall over on top of each other. He never spoke about it, and weeks passed before he cleaned it up. But Lorrie said it was best to pay no mind to it. She said anger comes with grief, and better Dad took his out on trees than on himself.

I stoop by one of the stumps and crouch low. Stubby shoots of new trees are already growing up from the inside. I pull Sary down close. "You be quiet," I tell her. She's not about to argue.

"We going after it?" Sary asks. She's got Tulip strangled, she's hanging on to her so tight.

"You're not afraid?"

"No. I'm not afraid. Let's go, James. Come on!" She's keyed up and practically popping out of her skin. "It'll be gone too far if we don't hurry."

I cross the fence first and start on the path to the creek. We're sneaking along as quiet as we can—like soldiers trying to creep up to spy on an enemy, me leading Sary, both of us stopping to

21

listen now and again. A cold, smoky dampness hangs in the air. Suddenly something rustles in the thicket up ahead, and Sary lets out a little squeal.

"There he is," she breathes, coming close to cling to the back of my jacket.

The dog's about twenty feet away, standing in the path and facing us. His tail sets into wagging, and right away I know we're safe.

He's bigger up close, but not scary. His eyes are brown and they're watching us, the same way we're watching him—thinking, sizing us up, like he's figuring if we're going to hurt him or not. Yesterday, from a distance, he looked darker than he really is. Most of the dark part is dirt. A whimper comes up from inside him. He wants to come to us, I can tell.

I go toward him real slow, one step at a time, holding my breath and praying I won't scare him off. But his ears tip up like he hears something, and he starts thinking about backing away. When I take another step, he turns fast and makes a dash for the creek.

I look back at Sary. "Come on," I say. She runs up behind me and we follow the dog deeper into the woods.

He's sniffing the ground, tracking to the left, then zipping off to the right. Every few yards he glances over his shoulder at us.

"Why's he do that?" Behind me, Sary's panting like a locomotive.

"To make sure we're following," I say, as if I know. "Come on, let's run faster."

We rush over the leaves on the floor of the forest, nearly floating we run so fast, dodging low branches, charging down the path after the strange gray dog. We come into the clearing above Devlin's Creek just in time to see him scramble down the bank, splash through the water, then vanish into the willows on the other side.

CHAPTER 4

Sary flops down on the ground, still gasping for air. I stand on the bank staring over the creek, tempted to follow but knowing better. Devlin's Creek marks the end of what's ours. No one crosses over that line, not even Lorrie.

Sary lies back with Tulip beside her. She stretches out in the leaves, crosses her arms over her chest, and closes her eyes.

"What the heck are you doing?"

"I'm dead," she says.

"Get on up from there, Sary." I need to be firm on this matter, otherwise she'll dive into a string of dying questions. Even though "dead" is a subject for lots of her questions, it's one I don't have a single opinion on.

I remember this one dark afternoon last February when Lorrie tried to explain to Sary that Mom was in Heaven, with Jesus. Since we've never been regular churchgoers, I knew right off my sister wasn't quite clear on who Jesus was. I'm sure for a time she walked around believing he was related to us somehow. Who knows what she thinks now? And I can't say if Mom's with Jesus or not. All I know for sure is she's not here with us. I kick up a pile of leaves and tell Sary she looks stupid.

"Quiet, James," she says in a somber, low tone. "I can't talk. I'm dead."

"No, you aren't. You're just acting empty-headed. Lorrie's going to skin you when she sees how dirty you are."

"Dirty doesn't matter when you're dead." She keeps her eyes closed and barely moves her lips when she speaks. I can tell she's doing this to make me nervous.

"Get up, Sary. It's not fit to play dead like that."

She opens one eye a little, then closes it again. "I'll be dead if I want. This is a nice place to be dead. It's cozy, like a nest. Do you think Mama would want to be in a nest? A nest is better than a grave, isn't it?"

She opens her eyes wide and stares up at me. I stare back.

"Well? It is, isn't it?"

25

"How should I know? Get up from there so I can brush you off."

"It's nice, James." When she runs her hand back and forth over the ground, the leaves make a whispering, ghostly sound. "Do you think it's nice being inside the ground?"

"Get off it now, Sary! I don't know dead and I don't know about lying in the ground, and if you don't get up from there I'm fetching Lorrie. She'll set you straight on it and you won't sit down till next week. She's going to spank you as it is."

"You know Lorrie doesn't spank." Sary gets up and tucks Tulip under her arm. "Why'd you say that?"

"Because if you were mine, I'd spank you."

"How come?"

"For being so dumb. Just see what you did to your hair. It's stuck all over with tree pitch and leaves."

Sary reaches to the back of her head.

"It'll never come clean," I say. "We'll have to cut your hair."

"Peanut butter," she says.

"What?"

"We can use peanut butter. That's what Mrs. Dowd used on Gilly when she got gum in her hair."

"Then we'd better hurry and get it done before Lorrie comes back from the store."

We run back along the path through the woods. At the fence I stop and take her by the shoulders. "Don't tell anyone," I say.

"I won't." She's touching her hair again. "Lorrie might get mad."

"No, not about your hair. Don't say anything about the dog, okay?"

"Okay, James," she says. "I promise. I won't tell."

Sary climbs onto the counter and takes the peanut butter from the cabinet. "Here, James. You rub it in. It'll work, you'll see."

But it doesn't, and when Lorrie shows up at the door with an armload of groceries, the kitchen smells like the school lunchroom and I have peanut butter stuck between my fingers and all over the back of Sary's head.

Lorrie pushes open the door, comes in, and sets the groceries on the counter. She folds her arms over her chest, then starts clucking her tongue as she walks toward us. Sary and I aren't about to move.

"Don't mind me," says Lorrie. "Go on with what you're doing. It looks delicious." Just like her to slide into a joke that way. And when she grins and asks for the recipe, I burst out laughing.

But not Sary. She bursts into tears.

Lorrie moves closer to examine her hair. Then her smile fades.

"James," she says, "fetch the shampoo. Don't forget a towel. And," she adds, "bring the scissors."

A little squeak comes up from inside Sary.

I find the shampoo and towel, but it takes me a few minutes of rummaging around in the sewing basket to locate the scissors. The whole time, I can hear Sary complaining downstairs, and when I get back to the kitchen she's bent over the sink and full-out sobbing.

Lorrie squirts shampoo into her hair and tries to console her, but Sary wails all the way through two washings. When Lorrie finally lets her lift her head out from under the faucet, my sister's face looks as if *it* got a scrubbing too.

"Stop your crying, hon." Lorrie wraps the towel around Sary's hair, then lifts her onto a stool. "If you stop, I think I can find a surprise for you when we're done."

"Do you have to cut it?" Sary sobs.

Lorrie starts combing. "Afraid so." She pulls the comb from the tangled wad at the back of

Sary's neck. "The peanut butter's out. But the pitch knots aren't."

Lorrie squares Sary in front of her on the stool, then starts in with the scissors. *Snip, snip, snip* is the only sound in the room as Sary's curls spill down onto the floor. I try not to think about what Dad's going to say when he sees what Lorrie's done.

With the comb in her mouth, Lorrie moves around to check Sary's bangs. They aren't exactly beauty-shop perfect, but she's done a decent job. She fluffs Sary's hair, then combs it again.

"Stay there," Lorrie says. "I'll be back in a minute."

"With my surprise?" asks Sary.

"With your surprise." Lorrie leaves the kitchen and heads down the hall to the stairs, then calls back to me, "James, how about sweeping the floor?"

I'm taking the broom from the closet when I hear the truck pull up into the yard.

"Is Daddy home?" Sary whimpers, reaching to cover her newly shorn head.

Dad's boots drop on the porch; then the kitchen door swings open. He comes in, rubbing his hands together.

"Chilly out," he says, blowing warm air on his hands. "Where's Lorrie? You two want to ride to the dump? I need to unload that old fence wire."

For about a second I wonder if he might not notice Sary's hair, but then he looks right at her and says, "What happened to you?"

I step between them, just praying Sary's not going to cry again. It's never any good to cry in front of Dad. "She got a haircut," I say.

"Mmmm." Dad moves past me to circle the stool where Sary's sitting. "Your aunt Lorrie do this?"

"Yes." Sary's voice quavers as Lorrie's footsteps come down the hall.

"We'll clip this in to keep your bangs . . . ," she's saying. Her voice drops and she stops dead when she sees my dad. She's got something in her hand. Right away I know it's Mom's silver barrette. But it's way too late to hide it. Dad's seen it too.

Quick as that, Lorrie tucks the barrette into her pocket and tries to act natural, as if she's only holding a pack of matches or a stick of gum. But we all know, even though no one says a word.

Sary's still all aquiver on her stool, and I'm aching for all of us, trapped here watching each other with that familiar, horrible quiet pounding down.

Dad's the first to move, turning his back to us and walking to the counter.

Then, almost like somebody else is moving her, Lorrie steps over to Sary and slowly takes out the barrette. "Like I said," she goes on as if Dad weren't even here, "this will hold your bangs back. It'll look real pretty, you'll see. Take Sary over to the mirror, James. Let her see how beautiful she is."

CHAPTER 5

We eat lunch together and no one mentions the barrette. I spend most of the time staring down at the orange and blue painted daisies winding around the rim of my plate, sure I'm not the only one who's thinking about Mom.

As usual, Lorrie does most of the talking. She says Mom's cousin Tim is coming to visit us sometime during the week, then goes rattling on about another woman in town who wants her to make more blue dishes. Right after we're finished, she hurries back to the housework, and we leave for the dump with Dad.

It's windy and cold out, so Sary and I have to ride up front in the cab. Like always now, we ride in silence—me by the window, Sary in the middle next to Dad, all three of us staring forward with that awful quiet rising up around us like some deep dark river.

All the way down the road I listen to the hum of the tires and the rattle of the load in the back, but the silence between us grows so loud I have to turn my face to the window.

I know it'll be all right once we get there and we're out in the open. Outside is always better. Outside, and daylight, and fresh air. Outside it doesn't seem to matter so much that Dad's about a million light-years away in his head, and that he's forgotten the easy way it used to be between all of us.

Going south the way we are, it's five miles to the dump turnoff. We pass by Wes Tiegland's acres of pastured sheep, and by the acres and acres of his dust-green alfalfa that stretch between Lorrie's house and town. A bit farther on we go by a few front yards where strangers look up, see us, but don't wave as we pass.

After Dad locked up our house in town and moved us out to live at Lorrie's place, I used to think it was this distance that kept me separate from my friends. I used to think the only reason I didn't see any of them was because I couldn't just walk out the back door and down the street to someone's house. But I've come to understand there's really lots more than ten miles of road between us and them. We're different since Mom died, outsiders now, living worlds away from the folks we used to know in town.

We turn off Route 5 at the stop sign, veer left, then bump along a gravel road for another mile or so before we finally come to the dump. A sign on the gate says BILLY NIGHTINGALE, CARETAKER. RING FOR SERVICE.

Billy lives inside the fence in a broken-down trailer some fellow parked and left about a century ago. He's usually in the yard raking garbage, or sorting tires and broken appliances. Sometimes he'll be resting in a shaggy old recliner out front, just sitting there thinking on his surroundings like an old man—except Billy Nightingale isn't old. He's only twenty-six, and I'm sure if anyone asked Lorrie, she'd say he's one of the best-looking men in the county. "He's such a great guy. I don't know why he stays all alone out there," she says—which I'm sure folks are starting to wonder about us as well.

I can't see Billy, but I can tell he's here by the spiral of smoke coming up from the stovepipe he's got wired to his roof. You have to honk before he'll come out and unlock the gates, but his dogs are always hanging around, usually gathered up in a nervous, bony bunch under some old wrecked car.

I get out to ring the bell, but before I reach it, the dogs spot me and set to barking as if Martians have landed. I count seven dogs, two more than Billy had the last time we were here.

Dad rolls the window down, leans out, and yells, "Ring it anyway. He won't come unless you do."

The jangle of the old bell kicks up the dog ruckus even more, and in a minute the door to the trailer creaks open. Billy sees us and waves.

"Hey there, Mr. Christie!" he calls out, grinning as he jogs over to open the gate. "Haven't seen you in an age! And you've brought the kids! Lorrie with you?" Every soul in town knows Billy has a near-critical crush on my aunt Lorrie. Sary and I figure that secretly she probably likes him too, at least as much as we do.

I help Billy lift the gates and swing them open; then Dad drives through and pulls up alongside us. Billy's peering into the back of the truck.

"Been busy tearing down fences?" he asks. Those eyes of his sparkle like two dancing blue lights. "Swing her 'round over there and I'll give you a hand."

Dad shoves the truck into reverse and backs up to the garbage pit. He stops the engine and gets out to shake Billy's hand.

Sary slides out after Dad and jumps to the ground. "You going to tell Billy about the dog?"

she asks. I'm not sure if she's asking me or Dad, so I glare hard at her.

Billy looks puzzled. "What dog?"

Dad explains about the stray. Sary comes over to stand by me and nudges me in the side to make sure I know she's not meaning to tell we saw it just this morning.

"Yesterday," Dad's saying. "Up where I'm working, on that fellow Navarro's place. You missing a dog?"

"Nope." Billy laughs, scanning the pack gathered around the truck. He spits on his finger, then begins counting. "Seven," he says. "That's how many I had yesterday so it's got to be right. I have to keep track of them, you know. Ever since last year, Wes Tiegland's been coming out here to make sure I keep them in line. What'd the dog look like?"

"Too big for a coyote," Dad explains. "Long hair. Dusty brown, some gray. White-tipped ears. Homely, and no doubt half starved, but a dog just the same."

Billy unlatches the tailgate. "James, you and Sary run along. I'll help your dad. I think there's an old bike by that bed frame over there."

Billy climbs into the back of the truck with Dad, rolls up the sleeves of his sweater, and begins tossing the wire into the pit.

"I'll keep a lookout for that dog," I hear him say. "I sure wouldn't want Tiegland to come across it. He'll shoot it for certain if he gets the chance."

"Then you'd be interested if I see it again? I know Lorrie doesn't want Wes to show up at her place any more than she wants a stray over there."

"Sure. If you see it, let me know."

Sary and I walk away. Pretty soon she's yanking on my arm.

"James," she says, looking down at the ground like she's about to spill a secret. "What if Billy tells Mr. Tiegland about that dog? He'll come shoot him with his gun, won't he?"

I tell her to hush up and forget about it. "You're crazy if you think Billy's going to say anything. He knows better. Besides, Mr. Tiegland's got more important things to do than chase after some stray dog he's never even seen."

"Then the dog will be okay?" Sary falls a few steps behind, then stops walking. Like always, she's waiting for me to say everything is going to work out fine.

"Sure, Sary. Come on, let's find the bike."

It's got a twisted frame and a flat tire, but it's good enough for Sary. She fools around on it for a while until Billy comes for us.

"Your dad's ready to go," he says, smiling with his eyes like he does. "He's looking pretty good. You all doing okay over at Lorrie's place?"

Sary and I nod. "We like it fine," I say.

"Well, I bet Lorrie's glad to have you there. Maybe I'll come out your way someday soon. You think that would be all right? Do you think Lorrie'd mind if I paid her a visit? Listen, do me a favor, will you?" Billy raises his hand. "Don't take off yet. I've got something . . . inside . . . Hang on. I'll be right back."

All seven dogs stick to Billy like bugs on flypaper as he trots over to his trailer. He comes back carrying a small box.

"Here. Give these to Lorrie for me, will you?" He kneels in front of Sary, holds the box out, and opens it. Bits of shiny colored glass blink in the sunlight.

"Nice, aren't they? Lorrie doesn't know, but I've been collecting them for her. Thought maybe she'd like to use them to decorate one of those pots." He closes the box, then runs his callused palm gently over it. "Can't sit here waiting forever hoping she'll take notice of me, can I? Got to do something sometime. Maybe this spot of coaxing will bring her around." He puts the box into Sary's hand and stands up. "Now go on, your dad's waiting. But listen. If you kids see that dog, stay away." When he looks down at us, his mouth is tight, his blue eyes suddenly serious. "You haven't seen it again, have you?"

Sary's turning away.

I shake my head. "No. No, sir. We sure haven't."

"Well, it might be dangerous; you never know. And don't feed it. You hear?"

"We won't," I say, steering Sary fast toward the truck.

Billy comes with us and walks around to Dad's window. "Give my regards to Lorrie. And, like I told the kids, if that dog comes by your place, whatever you do, don't feed it." He swings his arm in a wide sweep toward his pack of strays and chuckles. "You'll never get rid of it if you do."

CHAPTER 6

On Wednesday Mom's cousin Tim drives out from the city for lunch. Lorrie always goes to a whole lot of trouble to please him, probably because he seems to care more about us than most of Mom's family. Sary and I arrange the table in the dining room while Lorrie stays busy in the kitchen making chicken salad, French rolls, and Tim's favorite coconut cake for dessert. Dad even comes in early, and Tim arrives right on time, zooming up the driveway in his red Camaro like some crazy whirlwind.

"Heavy, yes. Breakable, no." He groans jokingly, staggering into the kitchen with an enormous cardboard box in his arms. He never shows up empty-handed. Last time Tim came for a visit, he left us with three years' worth of creamed corn he'd picked up at some warehouse sale. "Where should I put this?"

Lorrie laughs and directs him toward the counter.

Tim is a big man—as tall as Dad but heavyset and square, with a belly that pouches in a tight roll over his belt.

"What the devil's in that?" Dad asks, stepping out of Tim's way.

"Kiwis."

"Kiwis?"

"It's fruit. Neighbors raise them. Didn't realize they'd have so many." He hoists the box onto the counter, then reaches in and scoops out a handful of the fuzzy fruit. "Got a place for a few of these?"

Dad offers him one of Lorrie's new bowls. Bright green with violet stripes.

"Nice," says Tim, admiring it. "Sold any?"

"A few blue ones." Lorrie shakes her head casually.

Sary's on tiptoes and frowning into the bowl. She glances at me with an I-hope-I-don't-have-to-eat-them look on her face.

"You'll love kiwis," Tim tells her, then stoops to give her a hug. "They're sweet, like you." Sary gives him a big hug back.

"Getting taller," he says. "And Tulip-Virginia!

How glad I am to see you, sweet thing." He touches the top of Sary's head. "This was your mother's barrette, wasn't it?"

Sary's face pinks up at the mention of Mom.

"It's lovely. You got a haircut too."

"Lorrie did it," she says.

"Well, it's a fine job. And the barrette suits you. Melissa would have wanted you to have it."

Just like that, the kitchen goes quiet. I can almost feel the space between us tighten, as if everyone's taken a breath at the same time and sucked all the air out of the room. I can't believe it. In front of all of us, Tim has said Mom's name right out loud.

Sary's still beside him, clutching Tulip. His hand's still touching her hair. Across the room, Dad shifts from one foot to the other.

"We've got salad," Lorrie says, a little too loud. "Let's eat." She makes a wavy gesture toward the dining room.

Dad picks up the milk pitcher and leaves the kitchen. Sary's following him with the kiwis. I can't seem to move.

Tim picks up the basket of rolls, then turns to Lorrie, leaning his head close to hers, nearly whispering. "What's wrong? Don't you ever talk about her?"

I can feel myself shrinking against the cupboard. Lorrie turns to look over her shoulder at me.

"Keep your voice down, Tim."

"Keep my voice down? All I asked was if you ever talk about Melissa."

"Well, we don't. Okay?"

"You're kidding." He shakes his head. "And I suppose you're still not seeing that friend of hers either. The one who was driving the car? What was her name?"

"Isabelle. Dr. Isabelle Gamboni. And no, we don't see her. It's easier that way." Lorrie steps back from the counter and walks to the refrigerator, avoiding my eyes as she passes me. I know she wishes I would follow Dad and Sary to the dining room, but my feet stay planted to the floor like they've taken root.

"For Pete's sake!" Tim swings around. The rolls in the basket bounce. "Easier on who?"

"On everyone," Lorrie snaps back.

"It can't be easier on Isabelle. They were best friends. She was almost part of the family until the accident. Don't tell me Dan still blames her."

Lorrie doesn't answer but looks hard at Tim.

"You know," Tim goes on, "it's as if you're all pretending Melissa wasn't ever here. Explain to me how that can be easier on the kids?"

Lorrie's shoulders sag a little; then she says

softly, "I want them to remember their mother, Tim. I'm just not sure how to help them do it. Every time I try, I seem to make a mess of it."

Tim puts his free arm around her, looks over at me, and says, "I guess we'll just have to find a way then, won't we?"

Well, we're not even half through with Lorrie's famous salad before he tries out his remedy for helping us remember Mom. It starts when he mentions to Lorrie that the garden looks great.

"The kids keep it watered," she says. "That's the hardest part. All I do is start new plants. Too many, according to some people."

Dad's close to laughing when she says this. He's been after her forever to quit sticking stems in those little bottles. He thinks they clutter up the view out the kitchen window. "Seems *your* neighbors appreciate abundance too, Tim," he says, picking up a kiwi.

"Yes." Tim chuckles. "The Millers next door have covered a whole hillside with those damn things. Hope you like them. I know Cousin Melissa used to. She'd cut them in half and scoop out the middle. . . ."

As the meal goes on, so does Tim, mentioning Mom every chance he gets. Dad keeps looking out the window toward the driveway. Right now he isn't the only one who wants to leave.

Lorrie takes a try at distracting Tim by talking

about everything from rain forests to the recipe for her chicken salad. But while she's going on about people wanting to cut down all the trees in South America, Tim lowers his fork, looks straight at Sary, and says, "So much like your mother. So much like Melissa."

Sary squirms next to me, looking down at her plate without saying a word. My stomach's churning so bad I can't swallow anymore, so I just sort of push my lunch around with my fork. It seems like hours before Lorrie gives us permission to be excused.

"You kids clear your places," she says with a sour eye to my half-full plate. "We'll eat the cake later."

Dad stands up when we do.

"You're not leaving, are you, Daniel?" Lorrie asks. "So soon?"

He picks up his plate. "I'll help the kids clear the table," he says, following us into the kitchen.

Dad's scraping wilted lettuce into the garbage when the debate between Lorrie and Tim fires up again in earnest in the other room. I rinse my dish and try to hear over the sound of the running water. I catch snatches of the arguing, like Tim asking Lorrie, "What about their house in town? His job? Has he just given all of it up? And what about *you*? What about *your* future?"

"Be still, Tim. They'll hear."

45

I notice Sary moving close to the door. She's trying to listen too.

In the other room, a chair scrapes over the floor.

"He can't seriously be planning to stay here for good. He's going to end up like that Billy character the way he's cut himself off. . . ."

I crank off the water. Dad has his back to me, a dishtowel in his hand at his side. I turn my eyes away, trying to concentrate on the little bottles above the sink. The water in them makes the world outside look all ripply and pale. I don't move. Part of me wants to listen, part of me wants to run.

I know Lorrie never planned for us to stay with her so long, and sometimes I've tried to imagine us living back in town. But now I'm used to being here with her—used to her cooking, used to her voice, used to her watching over us when Dad goes out at night.

"Tim, you know as well as I do that Daniel can't raise those kids alone."

"Do I?" He clears his throat. "Perhaps it's time you let him try."

I feel that deep silence beginning to spread around us. Dad momentarily fills the emptiness with a clatter of silverware. I cough and slam a drawer.

Neither of us can stand it much longer. Finally

46

Dad reaches past me and puts the towel on the counter. "Go on out and play for a while. I'll finish this alone." He lifts a box of soda crackers from the shelf. "Take these. Doesn't look like we're going to get cake anytime soon."

CHAPTER 7

Sary crosses the pasture ten feet ahead of me, one hand clutching Tulip, the other clenched into a fist at her side. She stops by the fence, then spins around to face me. Her cheeks are wet with tears.

"It's because of me! Me and this stupid barrette!" She yanks it out of her hair. "Now Daddy will be angry and leave, won't he, James? And it'll be my fault."

Sary's right. At least about Dad leaving. He'll think of something he needs to do in town, just to get away.

She jams the barrette into my hand. "You keep it, James. I don't want to wear it anymore."

I know Sary felt proud when Lorrie gave her

Mom's barrette. And she wore it that first day when we went to Billy's without worrying at all about Dad. Come to think of it, I can't remember her being without it since.

She heads off in the direction of the cotton-woods. I run to catch up.

"Ah, come on, Sary. Lorrie gave it to you, and like Tim said, it ought to be yours. Quit fussing and I'll put it back in your hair. Nothing's your fault. You know as well as I do, Dad probably going to leave anyway."

I climb up on one of the stumps and make room for her beside me.

Sary lets me clip the barrette back into her hair; then she wipes her tears and looks away toward the house. "But what if he makes us go back to live in town?" she asks.

I can't bear to consider this. It's one of those times Sary needs me to tell her things will be all right, but I don't know how. Fortunately, for once, she doesn't have another question. So we just sit and eat crackers without talking for a while, munching and swinging our legs against the stump.

She's got crumbs pasted to her chin when she smiles up at me. "Let's go look for the dog," she says, jumping down to get a head start for the woods.

When we reach the clearing above the creek

Sary sets Tulip down on a log. The dog isn't here and I can see she's disappointed. I don't have the heart to tell her it'll be a true miracle if we see him again.

"Let's throw rocks," I say, trying to distract her. I put the crackers down and pick up a rock for Sary. She gives it a great heave-ho into the water.

I move away to stand in the open, facing the mountains on the other side of the creek, wondering . . .

"Come throw rocks with me," she says.

"In a minute."

Using my best form, I put two fingers up to my mouth, draw in a deep breath, and blow a long, rich whistle.

"Oh, do it again!" Sary says. "Make him come back, James! Do it again!"

Tucking my fingers between my lips, I whistle, then wait, then do it once more. But nothing happens.

Sary throws another rock. It dive-bombs into the creek with a hollow thunk as a cold wind sweeps down from the treetops, scattering leaves across the clearing. The chill comes up behind me to sting the back of my neck, reminding me that winter will be riding down on the valley soon. Winter and the wind. Winter and the cold. Winter and icy roads made invisible by blowing snow.

Winter and the memory of the night last year when Mom died.

A whirlwind flicks up a funnel of sand a few feet below us on the creek bank. Sary moves over beside me as I toss a stick into the water. Without talking, we watch it float downstream.

At first I'm sure it's just that same cold wind making the willows rustle on the other side of the creek, but suddenly, in a wild dash, the dog is bounding out into the open. He runs to the water, stops short of it, then woofs softly.

"He came!" Sary says. A truly amazed look lights up her face. "He really came!"

The dog woofs again.

"What kind of dog is he, James?"

"I don't know. I don't think he's any particular kind."

"Is he a hunting dog? He looks like a hunting dog. I'll bet he belongs to some big, whiskery man who likes to shoot rabbits and birds."

I creep a bit nearer the bank. The dog keeps his eyes on me, but he doesn't move. "I don't know if he's a hunting dog. But he's smart enough to be."

"How do you know?"

"Easy. A stupid dog would have starved to death by now."

"Make him come across," Sary says. "Whistle him over. Go on. He wants to, see?"

"Quiet, now. And don't move." The dog's tail flutters at the sound of my voice. Both he and I hold absolutely still, staring at each other. All around, the woods are silent except for the murmur of the wind, the trickle of water over the rocks, and, in the distance, the sound of a truck roaring to a start.

Dad's leaving. I glance at Sary.

The engine revs again. I look through the trees toward the house, then back at the dog. He's rigidly alert, listening, growing wary.

He begins to move away from the water, little by little, backing up toward the willows. Before I can whistle to stop him, he whirls around on his hind legs and scurries into the brush.

For a long time we stay on the bank, watching the place where he went. "That dog's too smart to let anyone but us see him," I tell Sary.

She sighs and takes Tulip from her perch on the log. "Come on, James. Let's go home now. Maybe we can have cake."

I'm about to follow her, but as I turn away from the creek I spot the box of crackers. I can't help myself. Something makes me pour what's left into a small pile on the ground. Sary walks back over to me, her grin about a mile wide. She takes my hand and we run up the path toward home.

CHAPTER 8

Cousin Tim is sitting on the living room floor with Lorrie, cross-legged in the middle of a clutter of photographs.

"Hey there!" he says. "Where have you been? We were getting ready to send a posse after you."

"We were at the creek," I tell him. "Dad left, didn't he?"

Tim nods. "He had errands to run. Said he'd be home by dinner."

I look away, knowing "errands to run" is the same as "fellow to meet" and "people to see." Dad won't be home by dinner. He won't be home by bedtime either. We probably won't see him until tomorrow afternoon.

"We've been waiting for you." Lorrie stretches out her legs. "Come see what Tim brought."

"Pictures?" asks Sary.

"Yes," Tim says, making room for the two of us on the floor. "Family snaps. Come see."

Sary and I sit down close to him. It's as if he and Lorrie have carpeted the floor with memories.

"Who took all these pictures?" I ask, wondering if Dad knows about them.

"Your father, mostly," Tim says. "And your grandparents."

Lorrie gets up to switch on the stereo. "We'll make a party of it. Daniel won't be home for hours. I'll light a fire and later we can have dinner right here on the floor."

"I thought Dan told you he'd be home for dinner," Tim says.

"He did, but I don't expect him."

"Why not?"

"He'll just stay out is all."

Tim shrugs. "You make it too easy for him."

"Don't start," Lorrie sighs, setting a match to a wad of paper in the fireplace. "You still don't get it, do you? He's my brother. Making it easy for him is my job. It's why he's here."

Sary is already sprawled on her stomach with a pile of pictures in front of her. I pick out a stack of my own.

Mom's in almost every one—high-school pictures, wedding pictures, snapshots of her when she was just a kid playing with her dog. And there are others too, more recent ones, of times that seem familiar. I'm in some. Sary and Dad are too. But some are just Mom—smiling from the porch of our old house in town; working at her desk; kneeling in the garden with dirt up to her elbows, laughing and trying to cover her face with her work gloves.

"See, Tulip," I hear Sary say softly, "that's Mama." She shows her doll the bright blue sweater that I remember Mom used to wear on cold mornings. Sary points out Mom's star-shaped earrings. The silver barrette.

"You were afraid to swim," I tell Sary, leaning in to show her a photo taken at the local pool we belonged to. Mom's sitting with her friend Isabelle, holding Sary, wrapped in a towel, on her lap. "The water used to scare you."

The pictures are bringing back things I'd forgotten, like Isabelle's sweet smile and the way Mom used to hold Sary like that, talking softly, until she stopped being afraid. I'm sure Mom must have been humming to her then.

"This was a good idea," Lorrie says, smiling in the firelight at Tim, then at Sary and me. She knows. She can see. Slowly, we're remembering.

It's long past Sary's bedtime when we finally finish. I figure since it's so late she'll fall straight to sleep, but she tiptoes into my room and taps me on the arm. She does this sometimes when she's had a bad dream, but I can tell by the look on her face that tonight is different. Like me, I think tonight she's just lonely.

"The wind's scaring Tulip," she says. "She wants to sleep in here."

I draw the quilt back and let her crawl in beside me.

"What was your favorite?" she asks.

"Favorite what?"

"Favorite picture."

"I don't know, Sary."

She tells me she liked Mom's junior-high picture best, because she could see her braces through her smile. "Did you see that one, James?"

"Yes, I saw it. Now go to sleep."

"James?"

"What?"

"Is it bad to cry for Mama?"

Another question I don't know the answer to. Maybe after almost a year it really is bad to cry. But I don't tell her that.

"It's not bad, Sary. Go to sleep, okay?"

I punch my pillow. I don't usually mind if she

falls asleep in my bed. Dad will sneak in after he comes home and take her back to her own room. Sometimes her company is even nice, but tonight I don't want to answer any more questions.

"What was his name?" she asks.

"Whose name?"

"The dog's. Mama's dog. The big gray one in the picture. Remember?"

"Foxy," I say. "I think Tim said his name was Foxy."

"He looked sort of like our dog, didn't he?"

"Our dog?"

"Uh-huh. I bet that was your favorite picture, wasn't it?"

I sit up and yank the covers off her. "Let me be, Sary. Stop asking questions or you'll have to go back to your own room. We don't have a dog. And I didn't have a favorite picture."

"Do you think he's lonesome? Or afraid? He's probably lonesome. But I bet he's not afraid. Do you think he ate the crackers?"

"I don't know. Go to sleep, for Pete's sake!"

She tries to be quiet, but I know her mind's still wide awake with wondering. "Well, do you *wish* he was ours?" she whispers.

I roll over and don't answer right away. "Sure," I finally admit. "But that won't happen."

"Billy Nightingale?"

"Him and whoever. Dad would never let us keep a stray. It would mean he planned to stay here."

"Maybe we could make Daddy like the dog," Sary says. "Then he'd *want* to stay here . . . like we do."

I look over my shoulder at her. She's practically breathing down my neck, she's so excited. "How?" I ask.

She curls in a ball beneath the quilt. "I don't know," she says. "You'll have to figure a way."

"We'll probably never see it again."

"Yes we will," she says. "I know we will."

Night shadows crawl up the wall. Outside, the wind stirs the branches of the buckeye tree. Beside me I can hear Sary's soft breathing and I know she's lying there awake, hanging on to Tulip and winding a strand of the doll's hair around her thumb.

I'm thinking about my old pajamas. The blue ones with the big white baseballs all over them. The ones I was wearing in that picture I can't get out of my mind. I was dressed for bed and sitting on Dad's lap with my head resting against his chest, his big hand resting on mine. I don't know why I didn't tell Sary it was my favorite. I guess because I don't think she'd understand, since Mom wasn't even in it.

"James? Are you awake?"

"Uh-huh."

"I miss Mama," Sary says.

"Me too," I tell her. "But sometimes I think I miss Dad even more."

CHAPTER 9

In the morning two sticks of Juicy Fruit are waiting on the kitchen table, along with the cold bacon and toast Lorrie left for us before she went to her workshop.

"Do you think Billy's right?" Sary asks. "If the dog ate our crackers, will he come back?"

"I don't know," I say, but inside I'm praying that what Billy said was absolutely true. Just in case, I stuff some bacon in my pocket. Sary eats all of hers but finds more crackers and two leftover muffins in the pantry.

She hums all the way to the creek.

I'm trying not to sound too excited, as if I don't care, when Sary points to the spot where we left the crackers yesterday. Even the crumbs are gone.

"Could have been birds. Or a raccoon," I tell her, even though somewhere inside I just know it had to be the dog. I don't want to set Sary up for disappointment, though, so I say, "Could have been anything."

But Sary doesn't buy this, and with a smile on her face as big as Christmas, she follows me to the bank above the water. I suck in a deep breath, pucker, then let out my loudest, longest whistle.

The dog comes so fast I bet he's been watching from the bushes the whole time, just waiting for us to call him over to eat more crackers. Like a rocket he shoots out of the willow brush, then comes splashing across the water. He stops smack-dab below us on the shore to shake the water off his back; then he looks up and practically smiles.

"Stay still, Sary. Don't move too fast or you'll spook him."

But this dog isn't the spooking kind, and he wags his tail about a million miles an hour when I climb down the bank to him. I go slowly and kneel at the bottom.

The closer I get, the shyer he is, just inching to me like a bashful little kid, one step, then another.

With Tulip buttoned up insider her sweater, Sary slides down the bank and scoots up close to me.

"It's a boy dog, isn't it, James? A dusty, dirty boy

dog." She says this real kindly, almost like she's trying not to embarrass him.

He might have ticks as thick as bees on clover, but I don't mind. "Here, boy," I say—like Billy would, as gentle and coaxing as I can. "I won't hurt you."

He must believe me because he takes the last few feet between us in a burst, hustles right up to me, then pushes his nose into my face. His big brown eyes seem so happy I put my arms around his neck and hug him. Oh, yes! There's no doubt now. I want him to be mine. He sniffs me all over, so I reach into my pocket and bring out the bacon. He gobbles it in one bite, then noses around for some more.

"Can I pet him?" Sary asks.

"Sure," I tell her. "He's friendly enough."

The dog sidles up and nudges her. Gingerly she touches him on the head. "He smells bad. But he's a nice dog, isn't he, James?"

"Sure he's a nice dog."

Sary pulls Tulip out of her sweater and holds the doll up to introduce her to the dog. When she puts her arm around him the way I did, he gives her one heck of a serious wet lick on the cheek. Sary tumbles over laughing.

"See! He likes me too," she squeals.

"Maybe." I shrug. "But he probably likes that jam on your cheek a whole lot better."

The dog paws Sary's knee, then sniffs her pocket.

She takes out one of the muffins she's brought and offers it to him. He's as polite as a starving dog can be, hardly touching her hand with his mouth when he takes it from her. And he's just as mannerly when she gives him the other one and the handful of crackers. I feel sorry I didn't think to bring more for him to eat, but he seems fine with it, almost as happy about the company as the food. When he's sure we don't have more, he crouches down on his front legs, his tail whipping from side to side.

Sary sets Tulip on the ground. "Can I throw a rock for him?"

"Don't you dare. You'd probably hit him in the head. Anyway, you're not supposed to let dogs go for rocks. It breaks their teeth."

"But he wants to play, James. Can't I do it once?"

"No." I get up and walk a ways along the rocky creek bank to find a stick. "Try this, Sary. See if he'll fetch it."

She tosses the stick, and the dog trots straight over and picks it up.

"Call him to you. See if he'll bring it back," I say.

"Here, dog! Come here, dog!"

Obediently he trots to her, drops the stick at her

feet, then sits down and waits for her to throw it again.

"He's smart, James. Just like you said."

This time Sary throws the stick as far as she can. The dog lopes over, sniffs around in the rocks, then brings it back.

"Does he think he's ours?" Sary asks.

"How should I know?"

"You said you wished he was. What if he wishes it too? And he knows how to fetch. That's useful, isn't it? Daddy might let us keep him if—"

"If nothing. According to Dad, a dog's just a nuisance. And what if we have to move back to town? We don't really live here, remember?"

"I remember," Sary says. "And a fetching dog wouldn't be good in town, would it?"

"No. But a watchdog might," I suggest, feeling brilliant.

"Watchdogs have to be mean."

"No, they don't. Any old regular dog can be one. Mrs. Lobonoff's got that puny mongrel named Trixie that guards the Laundromat downtown. All she had to do was teach it to bark when it heard stuff."

"Stuff like what?" Sary asks.

"Like burglars. Like footsteps."

"Whose footsteps?"

"Cut it out, Sary. You know, footsteps. If someone tries to sneak around outside the house at night.''

Quickly she stoops to take Tulip into her arms. "Is someone going to do that?''

"No. But if they did, and he was a watchdog, he'd know to bark and warn us.''

"That doesn't sound too useful to me if no one's ever going to do it.''

"Quit, Sary. You'll see. A watchdog is always useful, and I think we need one, so there.''

"Well,'' she says, twisting Tulip's hair into a ponytail, "even if you teach him, he won't be a watchdog.''

"Why's that?''

"How can he be a watchdog if he can't even come near the house?''

I don't try to come up with an answer to this question. Instead, I ignore Sary and invite the dog to sit down beside me.

He's a true mess. He looks like he's been roaming around in in the hills for weeks, and who knows what he's been finding to eat? By the way his bones are stuck out, I'm sure it hasn't been much. And it's clear it's been ages since somebody's cared for him. But with his ears all easy and his eyes half-closed, he lies down and lets me hunt around for burrs and ticks as much as I please.

We stay at the creek for a while, relaxing in the sun, me pulling ticks off the dog and Sary taking pleasure in smashing each one with a rock.

It's her idea that we ought to figure out a name for him. She says we can't just keep calling him "dog."

"But I bet he's already got a name," I say. "And he's not really our dog, is he?"

"I don't care. Let's give him a name anyway."

"We'll never be able to teach him—"

"Yes we can," she bursts in. "Like you said, he's smart. You want to call him Foxy? Like Mama's dog?"

"No."

"How about Trixie?"

"He can't be a Trixie. That doesn't suit him at all. It's a girl's name, anyway."

"Oh, yeah," Sary says.

"He needs a name like Max or Henry, a true dog name."

"I like Snickers. That's a nice name."

I laugh. "Sure, it's a nice name. For a candy bar."

Suddenly the dog jerks away from me. The hair along his spine starts rising up like a scrub brush as he moves out into the open to listen.

It's Lorrie. She's calling us to come home.

"Can we tell her? Let's tell her, James. Then he can be a watchdog."

I jump up and brush off my pants. The dog stays by me for a moment but then begins backing toward the creek.

"I'll tell her," Sary says. "You don't have to. I'll say it was me who fed him."

"Hush. We can't tell anyone. Not even Lorrie. She'd tell Billy. And she'd have to tell Dad."

Sary knows I'm right. Even if Lorrie didn't want to tell, we both know she'd feel obliged not to keep a secret from Dad.

Lorrie calls again and, fast as that, the dog turns to leave. Before we can stop him, he dashes across the creek.

As usual, he's disappeared into the willows on the other side of the water. Sary's beside me, hugging Tulip.

"I know what we can call him," she says softly.

"What's that?"

"Wander." She smiles up at me triumphantly.

I smile back.

CHAPTER 10

Wander. It's a fit name. And he's learned it in only a week, easy as that. Every minute we get free from chores, Sary and I take off to the creek to wait for him. All I do is whistle and he comes.

I've been carrying so many kitchen scraps in my pocket it's a wonder Lorrie hasn't figured we're up to something. But she never notices, busy as she is with more orders for pots and mugs.

I haven't told Sary, but as each day passes, it feels more and more like Wander belongs to us. To me. We're like matched laces, knotted and tied. Sometimes I lie in bed and wonder where he is, where he's made his nest for the night. And I imagine how it would be to have him for my own, sleeping on the floor by my bed, waking me in the morning with his cold nose in my face. Sary begs me to let her tell Lorrie, but I still have to say no. It's better to have a dog half the time than not at all.

Last night the radio said a storm was due, so this morning Dad left the house at dawn to help Aaron Navarro bring his sheep off the hills. Lorrie's kept us at chores since breakfast. Now it's noon, and it's finally started to rain.

Sary's got Tulip-Virginia propped up against the napkin holder on the table. She draws the window curtain aside, then puts her face up to the foggy glass. "I can't see anything out there," she says, rubbing her fist over the window.

It's raining hard. The barn and Lorrie's workshop are almost invisible. But I'm sure that even in this weather Wander will be waiting for us by the creek.

Sary's face is so close to the window, her forehead and nose leave a print. "He's all alone out there," she says. "He'll be hungry."

"Who's all alone?" Lorrie asks from the pantry door. "Who'll be hungry?"

"Ah . . ." Sary glances up at me, desperation clouding her face. One more time for me to put things back in order.

I grip her shoulder to keep her quiet. "Dad," I say.

"Oh, your dad will get wet, but he trailered

Heidi up the hill and packed himself a lunch. I expect he'll be home early." Lorrie pauses beside the table. "You feeling well, Sary? You seem glum today."

"She's fine," I say as I dig my fingers hard into her shoulder, wishing I had my hands around her throat.

"I'm fine," she agrees at last, smiling at Aunt Lorrie real innocent and turning to retie Tulip's hair ribbon.

"It's the rain," I say.

Lorrie nods. "Not much to do on a day like this."

"That's right," I agree. "Not much to do."

She grins. "Want to polish the silver? Change the beds? I'm sure I can find a floor for you to scrub."

"No, thanks," Sary and I say at the same time.

Lorrie puts on her clay-dusted rain slicker, then snaps the buckles one by one. "I've got pots in the kiln. If you go out, try to stay dry. The creek'll rise with the rain so don't go down there, okay?" Not waiting for a reply, she opens the door and heads outside.

"Come on," I tell Sary. "Get your raincoat."

"Where are we going?"

"To see if we can find him."

"But Lorrie told us not to go to the creek."

"We don't have to. If we call him from the fence, maybe he'll come."

"That's too close, James. What if somebody sees him?"

"Who's to see? Dad's way over at Navarro's, and you know as well as I do Lorrie will work until dinnertime."

Sary puts on her coat, runs back to the table for Tulip, then follows me out the door.

The yard smells of mud and wet grass. Water drips down our slicers in rivers as we slop across the flooded pasture to the cottonwood stumps. In the gray afternoon light the stumps look like giant swamp toads squatting by the fence. I remember again the day Dad cut those trees—a day just like this, rain pouring down, Dad all in a rage at Mom's dying.

At the edge of the pasture I lean against the fence and whistle.

"James?" Sary says.

"What?"

"Do dogs like the rain?"

"I don't know. I suppose it doesn't bother them."

Sary tells me she's sure they like it just as much as she does. She backs away from the fence, drops the hood from her head, and spreads her arms out wide. She spins in a circle, looking up into the gray sky and letting the rain splash onto her face. I remember Mom spinning Sary like that, Mom's hair trailing long and brown down her back and her laughter filling the air. I wonder if Sary's remembering too.

"This is fun, James." She giggles. "It tickles my face."

I let her dance that way until the rain has made puddles under her feet. Wander's not coming. I whistle again.

"Let's go," I say.

"But what about Wander?"

"I know a place. Maybe we can see him from there." I turn and lead her back toward the barn.

The musty smell of the barn is a comfort on dark, rainy days. I point to the loft above Heidi's stall and climb the ladder after Sary.

"There." I motion to the big double doors at the end of the loft. Sary scoots across the hay-strewn floor on her hands and knees.

I lift the wooden latch, and with a deep moaning creak the hay doors swing open to a view of the pasture and the woods beyond. In the distance, through the trees, I spot the place where the path drops down to the creek.

Over and over I whistle. Then we lie on our stomachs in the hay, watching through the rain and waiting.

After a while Sary rolls onto her back and asks me if I think Wander's gone home.

"No," I say, as much to convince myself as her. "He's only waiting for the rain to stop."

"But what if he's dead, James? It's cold. I bet he froze. What if he got washed away?"

"He's not dead, Sary. He's probably hiding someplace, staying dry. He'll be back, you'll see."

I turn over and stare up at the open rafters of the barn. A swallow swoops low and rises, lighting above us on a high crossbeam. Inside, I'm praying I'm right. Praying I know what I'm talking about. Praying Wander's safe and he'll come back to us.

"It's cozy here," Sary says, closing her eyes. She starts breathing slow and easy, and I figure she's gone to sleep or is playing dead again.

Then she says, "Do you think Wander's got a nest in his hiding place?"

"I suppose."

"So he's cozy too?"

"Sure, Sary. He's cozy too."

It's raining hard. We don't speak for a while but just lie side by side listening to it pound down on the roof. Sary's humming right along.

"Is this like Heaven?" she asks.

When I look over at her, she smiles.

"It must be close," I say. "Real close."

CHAPTER 11

I'm happy just lying here, but Sary can't stay still any longer.

"Teach me to whistle," she says, sitting up and poking me in the arm. She puckers her lips and blows a stream of spit in my direction.

"Cut it out! You don't do it like that. You're not supposed to spit."

"Well, teach me then," she says. "I want to learn."

"You go like this." I blow a slow, rising tune that swings real easy around the inside of the barn. Sary is impressed.

"Show me! Show me!" she begs.

"What's so danged important about learning to whistle?"

"I want to make a tune, like Lorrie does when she's working. And I want to call the dog like you do. I want to call Wander, James. Please, teach me."

I sit up and kneel in front of her so she can see. "Your lips are only part of it. It's mostly what you do with your tongue that makes the sound."

I try to get her to pucker up, to tuck her tongue against her bottom teeth, but she can't get it right.

"I can't do it," she whines, all vexed and flustered like she gets when things aren't working the way she wants.

"Ah, Sary. You've got to figure it out by yourself. It's *your* tongue." I stick mine out and wag it at her, hoping she'll laugh. But she doesn't.

"Don't tease, James. I want to learn."

"Then you have to practice. That's how come I know how."

So she practices and practices. She practices until it's almost dark, until she nearly drives me nuts and I close the hay doors and tell her I'm going back to the house.

I'm heading for the ladder just as Dad's truck rumbles into the driveway, the horse trailer banging along behind it. Dad pulls up in front of the barn, idles, then stops. I hear the door to Lorrie's workshop squeak open, then close.

Lorrie calls out to him, "Hey there, Daniel!" I

hear her boots slosh through the mud. The truck door opens.

"Long day?" Lorrie asks.

"The longest," Dad answers. I look back at Sary, then sit down at the top of the ladder.

Lorrie says, "The kids were worried about you. It's been rotten here all day."

"Up on Navarro's place too. Wind made it worse."

"I've closed up shop for the night, so we can eat early. Leave the horse. You look tired."

"Maybe because I've been chasing sheep in and out of gullies all day," he says. "Kids okay?" The bolt rattles on Heidi's trailer. The gate drops to the ground with a hard thud.

"They're fine, I suppose. Haven't seen much of them today. I've been too busy. Like you."

Heidi's hooves clatter on the trailer ramp.

"And what is that supposed to mean?"

"Nothing," Lorrie says. "Nothing at all."

Dad clears his throat. "Does it mean you agree with Tim?"

Sary crawls close and taps me on the arm. She's trying to tell me we should leave, and I know she's right. This talk is none of our business. But curiosity makes me shush her so I can listen anyway.

"Agree with what?" Lorrie asks.

"That we shouldn't be staying here. That we shouldn't rely on you so much."

"I never said you shouldn't stay here. You and the kids can stay forever as far as I'm concerned."

"Well, they *are* attached to you now," Dad says. "They need you."

"Oh, come on, Danny. You know I'm not what those kids need. I can feed them, and keep them clean, and I can certainly love them. But . . . I can't be their mother."

Over Heidi's pacing I hear Dad say, "I can't be their mother either."

"Of course you can't," Lorrie says. "But you could try being their father. You used to be good at it, you know."

I can feel that same old silence now, seeping through the walls of the barn, then spilling like ice water into my stomach. The door to the trailer slams.

"It's late, Lorrie," Dad says. "And I'm beat. I'll be up for dinner in a while."

Hail has begun to batter the tin roof of the barn. Sary's moved up so close to me she's practically pushing me off the ledge. Below us the door creaks open and Dad switches on the light. Without a word, we watch him lead Heidi into the barn and take off her saddle.

We shouldn't stay up here, hiding like this, but I

don't want to go down there now and see the troubled expression I know will be on his face, especially when he discovers we've been listening.

So we keep quiet as he goes back out into the storm for his toolbox. He brings it in, sets it on the floor near the workbench, and starts to put his tack away—bridle on the wall, halter beside it, saddle and blanket on the rack by the stall.

If someone asked I couldn't explain it—Dad isn't doing anything special, only ordinary chores—but for some reason I feel good just watching, almost like I'm watching him the way he used to be.

Sary makes a move like she's going to say something to him, but I pull her back and lean against the post at the top of the ladder. The hail has stopped; now only a soft shower is pattering the roof overhead.

Dad takes Heidi's brush from the shelf, holds it for a moment, and then, without using it, reaches up and puts it away.

A sudden gust of wind whistles through the walls, sending the bulb that lights the old barn swinging back and forth. Below us, Dad's shadow moves from side to side over the floor. Heidi steps up close to him, whickering softly as he coaxes her into the stall right below us.

Her hoof makes a heavy clunk on the wooden floor as she takes another step toward her grain bucket. While she eats, Dad walks up beside her and runs his hand along her neck, then over the gentle curve of her spine. It makes me ache inside, and I have to shake off the urge I'm feeling to climb down there and stand by him in the warmth of that big mare—stand beside the soft, comfortable father I used to know.

Heidi nudges him in the shoulder with her nose. Dad lowers his face and lays his cheek against her back.

When I realize he's crying, I can't make myself turn away. Even when Sheriff Whipple came to tell us about Mom, even at the funeral, when our hearts were white-cold and breaking in that December wind, I can't remember ever seeing Dad cry.

"Melissa."

It's like her own ghost, Mom's name floating up to me and Sary. It hangs over us. I can feel Sary's fingers tighten around my arm as Dad steps away from the horse and turns to look behind him. He seems almost startled, like he didn't mean to speak Mom's name at all.

Suddenly I notice how hard Sary's clinging to my arm. I take her hand and gently pull her back from the ledge with me, embarrassed beyond all knowing that we've spied on Dad—worse, that we've seen him cry.

After a moment or two I hear the stall door

close, then the hollow sound of Dad's boots cross-ing the floor. The light switch clicks; the barn darkens; the door opens, then closes. Finally I hear his footsteps passing slowly around the out-side, toward the back of the barn. Though it's safe for us to leave now, Sary and I just sit in the dark, listening for a while, until all we can hear is the warm, rhythmic, ordinary sound of Heidi chewing her dinner.

CHAPTER 12

The patter of leftover rain dripping from the buckeye trees follows us on the path from the barn like small, steady footsteps. In the sky, a cluster of stars is trying to blink out from behind the clouds.

I kick my boots off on the porch. I'm pulling off Sary's when Lorrie opens the door.

"Where have you been?" she asks. "I was about to worry. I could have used some help with dinner. Have you seen your dad?"

"No." I shake my head, grabbing tight to Sary's foot. I give her a look so she'll know not to say anything.

"Well, the soup will keep. We can wait." Lorrie stays in the open doorway, gazing in the direction of the barn. I know it's Dad, not us, she's really been worried about. "I'm sure he'll be here any minute," she says. "Come on in."

By the time Dad finally shows up we're at the kitchen table. He goes straight to the sink to wash. Lorrie walks up behind him and waits for him to finish drying his hands; then she puts her arms around him. "I'm so sorry," she says.

I'm expecting that familiar quiet to fill up the room, and I wonder how I'll ever make it through the whole meal without looking Dad in the eye—sure if I do, he'll see I know he's been crying, and then I'll either go red and show my shame or burst out crying myself.

I can tell Sary's nervous too, because she's gone weirdly silent. Come to think of it, the last time she asked me a question was ages ago—way before . . .

As Dad walks to the table, I'm working hard to come up with something clever to say. But as it turns out I don't have to. He puts his hand into his pocket, pulls out a blue jawbreaker, then sets it on my plate. He takes out a green one for Sary.

"After dinner," he says, sitting down across from us.

He makes a point of complimenting Lorrie on the dishes. Tonight they're yellow with orange birds perched in a ring of ivy leaves around the rims. Lorrie thanks him; then dinner goes right on as usual, as if nothing's happened. By dessert Dad's eyes are almost cheerful and I feel like maybe I dreamed the whole thing in the barn.

I guess Sary's relaxing too. She makes the announcement that she can whistle and puckers up to show everybody. She blows softly and a high, airy sound comes out. Dad smiles at her, obviously pleased.

"Where did you learn that?" he asks.

"James taught me. I'm almost as good as him already."

"That so?" Dad says. "He must be a good teacher."

Lorrie glances up from her plate, nods, then smiles at Dad.

Full of herself now, Sary blows once more. This time a clear, sweet note floats through the room.

"I'm going to whistle for the dog," she says.

Like a shot, I swing my foot out to knock her in the knee. "Dog?" Did she really say "Dog?"

"Speaking of dogs," Dad says, "I saw Billy in town today."

I keep looking down at the birds on my plate, but I stretch my leg as far as I can and give Sary a second whack.

Lorrie gets up and walks to the counter. She comes back to the table with a bowl of fruit and a knife, then sits down and begins peeling and eating a kiwi just as casually as you please. I'm hoping she isn't in the mood to hear about Billy, but she asks, "Did he say he's coming this way?"

"He told me he might," Dad says. "Just to see you."

Lorrie almost chokes on her kiwi. "Billy didn't say that!"

"To be honest, he didn't. He told me he wanted to search for that dog we saw the other day."

I try to give Sary another warning with my foot, but she's caught on and moved her legs out of reach.

"He said he'd be by in the next day or two. Tiegland's been after him. Accused him of letting his dogs run wild. Told him a dog's been killing his sheep."

"Well," Lorrie mutters, "if that's so, it'll soon be a *dead* dog. Whether Billy likes it or not."

I glimpse Sary out of the corner of my eye. I can see fear rising on her face. She looks positively like she's about to throw up.

Maybe it's what Lorrie said to him, or maybe it's just the storm that's keeping Dad home tonight. The wind has come up and is blowing hard, banging the shutters against the house. Sometimes it blows so hard it brings the electric lines down between us and town. If that happens, the dark will send us all to bed early. But for now, Sary's snuggled up by the fire changing Tulip's hairdo, and I'm sitting on the floor watching television and trying to forget—about Dad crying in the barn, and about Wes Tiegland and his dead sheep.

Dad opens the newspaper and tries to get comfortable in his chair.

He's just about to settle into reading when a sudden gust rattles the windows. It fills up the room worse than our usual quiet and makes him fold the paper and stare out into the dark.

Wind always makes Dad jittery. Maybe because it reminds him of that night last year when the sheriff came. I remember I was sitting on the floor just like this, leaning against our old red couch, when I looked up and saw the sheriff through the open doorway, his face lit in shadows by the dim porch light. And I remember Dad's face too, pale as ashes when he told us what the sheriff had said.

Mom died on the highway. I've never been brave enough to ask the exact spot of the accident, and so far, no one's offered to tell me. But I'm sure it must have happened on that big turn, the one up on Juniper Pass.

I remember, earlier that stormy night, when Mom's best friend, Isabelle Gamboni, came by to pick her up. They were going to the movies over in the city. Mom put on her coat, then kissed me and Dad and Sary good-bye. She went out the door smiling, but she never came back.

It hurts to think about now, with the wind rattling the windows like the devil himself is trying to get in. It hurts to think about her being gone forever, knowing that Dad's a million miles away too, even though he's right here—so close that if I turned and held out my hand, I could touch him. But when Sheriff Whipple came by later that terrible night and told us about Mom, Dad followed him out the door into that storm and *he* never really came back either. The only difference in their going seems to be that at least when Mom left, she had remembered to kiss us good-bye.

The electricity doesn't go out, but Lorrie sends us to bed early anyway. It's a relief to be upstairs, doing something boring and regular like brushing my teeth. I make it last as long as I can, then head down the hall. When I pass Sary's room, she's standing by the window.

"What are you doing?" I ask.

"Just looking," she says.

"At what? It's way too dark—"

"Is Wander out there?" she asks. "Sometimes it feels like he's watching. Like he can see us, even though we can't see him."

It makes me shiver to imagine Wander's night-yellow eyes shining back at us through the dark. He could be watching us, but after hearing about Wes Tiegland and his dead sheep, I'm almost hoping he's gone. I walk to the window and stand beside Sary.

Below us, the porch light flicks on and the screen door creaks open. I hear Lorrie say, "Be gone as long as you want. We'll be fine."

I look down into the yard, hear the door close, then see Dad's shadow pass along the front walk in the beam from the porch light.

"He's leaving again," Sary says.

Lorrie and all the other relatives told us, "Give your dad time. Give him space." But what good has it done? The more time that's passed and the more space we give him, the farther and farther away he seems to go.

A thin, spiny shadow of a branch sways back and forth beneath the buckeye tree. The truck sputters to a start. Sary moves close to me and we watch Dad's taillights move down the driveway until they fade into nothing more than two red specks in the distance.

"Make him come back," she says. "Make him come back, like Wander."

"I can't," I have to tell her. "I don't know how."

CHAPTER 13

By morning the storm's passed, and when Sary and I go outside in the sunshine the world looks a whole lot better than it did last night. New grass is poking up everywhere and the sky's bluer than I've ever seen it. Sary's walking ahead of me along the path to the creek, humming in that soft way of hers.

When we reach the clearing, I walk to the edge of the bank above the water and let out a long, shrill whistle. It sails into the woods on the other side.

"He probably went home," Sary says.

"And where's that, do you suppose?" I ask her.

"He'll come. You'll see."

She hugs Tulip and I see disappointment creeping up on her face. I feel it some too, but fear keeps me from believing Wander's gone. I have to think he'll come, so I whistle again. Then Sary does too.

We wait, watching the brush beyond the water for any sign of him.

It's longer than usual but Sary's managing patience. She stays quiet beside me, just digging a trench in the mud with her toe. Right now it seems like Wander's come to mean more to us than almost anything else in the world.

My confidence begins sliding away just as Sary gasps, "Yes!" and Wander bounds out of the brush and across the creek.

Dripping wet and way dirtier than before, he scrambles up the bank, runs straight over, and jumps on me. He licks me on the cheek, and as Sary watches, a wild, glorious grin lights up her face.

"I told you he'd come back!" I nearly shout, not minding in the least that Lorrie's going to pitch a fit when she sees how dirty I am. Right now, Wander is our dog, and that's all that matters.

As he eats the sandwich I brought, Sary and I sit on the log with Tulip between us, the sun warming our knees. When Wander finishes he sits politely in front of Sary, waiting for the treat she has for him. He eats the corn bread eagerly, licking the last crumbs from her hands before he comes back to me, sniffing around my feet and up my legs.

"No more," I say. He yips and jumps sideways.

Sary laughs. "He wants to play!" She gets up, finds a stick, and tosses it. It wobbles in the air for a few seconds before it lands below us beside the water.

Wander races down the bank and brings it back, dropping it with a soft plop in the mud at my feet.

Sary picks it up and throws it again, but this time Wander's not paying attention. Something by the alder tree on the other side of the clearing has caught his eye. I walk over to investigate.

"It's a bird's nest. Must have fallen out of the tree." I pick it up and hold it out for Sary to see.

"Put it back, James. Poor birds. Where will they sleep?"

"It's an old one, Sary. The wind must have knocked it down last night. No birds will use it now. They're probably gone anyway. I bet they left it ages ago."

Puzzled, she looks up into the sky. "Where did they go?"

"South, I think. Some birds leave for the winter."

"Will they come back?"

"Sure." I give the nest to her. "Sometime in the spring. Let's go down to the water."

"Well, where will they sleep when they come home?"

I sigh and stop halfway down the bank. "They'll build a new one, Sary. Now, come on."

Cradling the nest carefully in one hand and using the other for balance, she follows me down the bank. At the creek she parks herself on a rock to examine the nest.

"There's sticks and grass in it," she says, running her finger over the rim. "And string. Look, James. The birds used hair too!"

"So? Birds make their nests from lots of stuff."

She raises it up in the sunlight. "Look at it, James."

Wander's impatient for another game of fetch, but to humor Sary I walk over to check out the nest. "It's nothing special, only horsehair," I say.

"No it's not. See, James? It looks like Mama's."

I pick up a stick and throw it hard at the water. Wander splashes downstream after it. "That's stupid, Sary. You don't know that."

"Yes I do. It *is* Mama's. I can tell."

"It's just a dumb old bird's nest, Sary."

"No it isn't!" she snaps back at me.

Wander retrieves the stick, then comes to sit in a sunny spot by my feet. I kneel and stroke him behind the ears.

"Listen, Sary. That could be anybody's hair, someone who lived here twenty years ago."

Ignoring me, she stands up and twirls in a slow circle, holding the nest out in front of her. It glistens red, then gold, then a familiar deep rich brown.

"It's not hers!" I practically holler, trying to snatch the nest. "It's no part of Mom!"

"It is so if I want it to be!" Sary yells back, shoving me aside and hurrying away. Wander gets up and prances after her. I wait for a moment, then follow them up the bank to the clearing.

At the top I see that Wander's standing nervously beside Sary, sniffing the wind.

"What's he smelling?" Sary asks.

"How should I know?"

Wander trots toward the path that leads to the house. Then he stops and tilts his head to listen.

"Look at him, James. He hears something."

The hair along his neck bristles. And he's tucked his tail down tight against his hind legs. He bares his teeth and snarls.

"I don't like that, James. Make him stop. He's scaring me."

I walk over, stoop down beside Wander, and wrap my arms around his neck. Then I hear it too: a low drone, then the clank of shifting gears as a truck slows to make the turn from Route 5. Someone's coming to our house.

I know by heart the particular rumble of Dad's

truck. This isn't it. The engine idles loudly at the gate.

"Who is it, James?"

Wander pulls away and walks just ahead of us as I grab Sary's hand and start along the path to a place where I can see the house through the trees.

A beat-up blue flatbed truck's parked in the driveway.

"Get down, Sary! It's Billy Nightingale!"

"What's he want?" she says, worry in her voice.

"He must have come about . . ." The truck door slams and Wander growls again. I crouch down and put my arm around him. "We have to go up to the house."

"But what about Wander?" Sary's voice is near panic. "He can't be so close. What if Billy sees him?"

Wander licks my face. "He'll leave like he always does. Come on, let's start walking. He'll go back."

I can see Billy now. He's leaning casually against his truck, watching Lorrie walk up the path from her workshop. She pulls off her bandanna and waves to him.

Wander smells the air and listens, but his tail is beginning to swing. He's not afraid anymore. Now he's just curious.

"He wants to go with us," Sary says. "What'll we do?"

I point Wander toward the creek. "Go home," I say firmly. "Go on." He cowers but doesn't budge.

"Don't be mad at him, James. He's just being a good watchdog. I'll stay here with him."

"Oh, sure, that'll work fine. What am I supposed to say when Billy and Lorrie asks me where you are? You want me to tell them I left you alone by the creek?"

She shakes her head. "Then you stay," she says. "Let me go—"

"And let you spill the beans? What will you say when they ask where I am? And what if they ask about *him*? Just hush up and let me take care of it."

Wander trembles beside me.

I lead him back to the clearing, step away, and wave my arm at him. "Go! Go on, now!" He shrinks down and whines.

"Stop it, James!" Sary cries out, running up behind me. "You're being too mean."

"Get away! Go on!" I pick up a stick and raise it over my head, but Wander thinks I'm playing. He wags his tail.

I raise the stick again.

"Don't hit him!" Sary yells. "You're not going to hit him, are you?"

"Back off, will you, Sary? Let me handle it. And don't make so much noise, or they'll hear you."

"But you can't hit him!"

"I'm not going to hit him," I say. "I only want to make him go away. It's for his own good. You go ahead. I'll catch up." I give her a little push up the path and she stumbles away, looking back every few seconds to see if I'm coming.

Desperate, I shake the stick hard, hoping it will scare Wander off. "You'd better get moving if you know what's good for you!"

I hear Lorrie. Wander does too, and he seems ready as ever to see who's calling out our names. He takes a step in my direction, then another. He wants in the worst way to follow Sary, I can tell. I shake the stick at him again and he stops, then keeps on coming. It's panic that makes me pick up a rock.

"No!" Sary shrieks. "You can't!"

I glare over my shoulder at her. But it's too late. Lorrie and Billy must have heard her scream. Through the trees I can see them coming across the pasture.

Sary looks at me helplessly. I look back at Wander only long enough to wheel around and send the stone flying.

It hits him square on the side with a hard whack. He doesn't yelp, but he stares at me, surprise filling his eyes. He stays there for a bewildered second before he whips around and races toward the creek.

Behind me, Sary is crying. I run to her, grab her by the arm, then try to drag her toward home. But she pulls away from me and takes off alone, her feet slipping sideways in the mud as she runs.

Lorrie and Billy are crossing the pasture at a fast clip now. Sary beats me to the fence and stops to wipe her tears.

"There was nothing else to do," I try to explain—more to myself than to her. "And it won't help if you're crying when they see you."

"He won't come back," she sobs. "I just know he won't. This time he's gone for good."

CHAPTER 14

Billy sees us now. "There they are! Hey, kids!" he calls out, and waves. Lorrie stops by the cottonwood stumps.

When she sees my shirt, she sets her hands on her hips. "What happened to you?"

I lie and tell her I fell. "It was an accident."

"I thought I heard somebody scream," Lorrie says as Sary and I cross the fence. I frown over at Sary, but she's not looking at me.

"We were down by the creek," Sary says. "It was slippery. It wasn't James's fault. He was trying to help me get this." She still has the nest. She holds it out for Lorrie to see.

"Very nice," Lorrie says impatiently, steering us

toward the house. "But maybe you shouldn't play there when it's wet. Just look at you!"

Billy chuckles when he takes note of how dirty I am. He's never too cleaned-up himself unless he's visiting. Today it looks to me like he's even shaved. "Settle down, Lorrie," he says, laughing. "It's only a little mud. It'll wash out." He moves up next to us to rest his arm on the fence behind Lorrie.

She smiles at him, then turns to finish her scolding. "Fine," she says. "But you guys scoot into the house and get cleaned up—"

"If you don't mind," Billy interrupts, "I wanted to ask the kids about something."

"Oh?" Lorrie smirks. "Is *that* why you drove all the way out here?" She turns back to him, leaning over the fence to snap off a sprig of pink geranium.

Billy winks at us, then reaches out to gently wipe a patch of dried clay from Lorrie's cheek. "Only partly," he says. "Do you kids remember that dog you told me about the other day? Have you seen it again?"

I step in front of Sary, since there's no table to hide my nudges this time. "No, sir," I say. "Just that once up in Mr. Navarro's field."

"That's too bad. I suppose I didn't really expect it to be this far down the valley, but I was hoping."

"Why's that?" Lorrie asks.

"I thought I might be able to get to it before that crazy Wes Tiegland does. He was out at my place this morning. Said he lost one of his best ewes last night. Even though he's been losing stock to predators for years, he's convinced the culprit's that dog your dad told him about. As it usually is with Tiegland, a stray's the easiest thing to blame."

Sary stays behind me, one foot to the other. She's fighting the urge to blurt out all she knows about Wander. I'm fighting hard not to say that I'm sure he didn't kill stupid old Wes Tiegland's ewe.

Sary can't keep it in any longer. "He didn't kill any sheep," she says.

Billy peers past me. "You know something you're not telling, Sary?"

I step backward onto her foot and laugh. "She's full of stories. We only saw it that one time."

"You sure?"

"Yes, sir," I say. "I'd remember if I saw that dog again. We only saw it once, honest."

Billy accepts this, but Lorrie isn't quite so ready to believe me. She leans down close to Sary's face and asks gently, "Sary? Have you seen that dog again?"

Poor Sary. I know she's dying to tell. She takes a deep breath. "No, ma'am," she says in her most serious voice, one even I'd be proud of. "Not ever again."

"Well, fine." Lorrie pats Sary's shoulder. "Then go into the house and clean up. I'll be there in a little while. I want to show Billy what I made with those bits of glass he sent over."

"Bet it's classy, whatever it is," he says, smiling at Lorrie.

"It's only a flowerpot. But come with me; it's in the workshop. You kids run along."

As we walk away, Sary turns and says to Billy, "We'll tell you if we see the dog again."

I push her ahead of me toward the house.

Sary's still clutching the bird's nest. I wait for her to sit down on the porch step; then I stand in front of her to pull off her boots.

"Pee-yew!" she says, wrinkling her nose. "Something stinks!"

She's right. Something does—and it's not just her socks or boots. Both of us reek all over like wet dog. I remark that it's a wonder the smell didn't give us away.

"You should have let me tell," she says. "Lorrie wouldn't get mad."

"That's not the point, Sary. If Wander's going to be ours, we have to keep him a secret, remember?"

"Is it okay to lie to keep a secret?"

"I don't know." I tug hard on her boot. At first

the lying felt right, but now it seems like the longer we keep our secret, the farther away from the truth we get. "Listen, Sary. It's just better if we keep still about Wander. Nothing's going to change the fact that Wes Tiegland thinks he killed his sheep. And if we told anybody, Wes would be sure to find out; somebody'd have to tell him."

Sary looks away and begins picking at the burrs in her socks. "Well," she says, "it doesn't matter anyway. Wander's not ever coming back. Not since you hit him with that rock. He hates us now."

I toss my boots into the corner, kick hers aside, and go into the house. I let the door slam behind me.

It's not until much later, after dinner, when Dad's gone, that I speak to Sary again, and that's only because she comes charging into my room with a full-blown case of hysterics.

"What the heck's the matter with you?" I step to one side to let her by.

"I don't have Tulip-Virginia," she sobs, stumbling over to my bed and collapsing. "I left her . . ."

I shut the door, then go over to sit beside her. "I've told you a million times to keep track of her, Sary. What'd you expect? You were bound to lose her."

"I didn't say I *lost* her, James." She sits up and

wipes her face. "I said I *left* her. At the creek. I know where she is. I put her on that big log. Remember?"

"No. And like I said, it was bound to happen sometime. Come on, don't cry. Go to bed. You can get her tomorrow."

"I can't leave her out all night. I'm going to tell Lorrie. She'll help me." Sary starts to get up, but I push her back down on the bed.

"No you're not," I tell her sharply. "What if she goes down there and finds Wander?"

"But Tulip's all alone." Sary lies down and jams her face into the pillow. "I have to get her now!"

"Ah, don't be a baby. She's only a doll. It's not like she's alive or anything. She doesn't know the difference. And stop crying or Lorrie will hear you. You've caused enough trouble with your crying today. If you quiet down, I'll let you sleep in here, okay?"

"I won't sleep, James. I can't sleep without Tulip."

"Then don't sleep. Just pretend. Get under the covers and be quiet. Any more crying and you're on your own."

"F-F-fine," she agrees, trying to muffle her sobs in my quilt.

She doesn't stop crying for a long time, not until I'm sure she's used up all her tears and has fallen asleep. I'm still awake when Dad's truck rattles through the gate and into the yard.

His boots drop softly onto the front porch. He opens the door slowly so it doesn't make too much noise, then eases it shut behind him. As he crosses the kitchen floor, I can barely hear him. He's walking as quietly as he can, catlike, in his socks. Now the stairs creak beneath his weight.

Sary must be asleep, because she doesn't budge or make a sound as Dad comes into the room. I try to breathe slowly so he'll think I'm sleeping too, but I open my eyes a little to see him.

He's right next to the bed. He's not doing anything but standing there, watching us like he'd watch a sunset—just staring down on me and Sary like we're hills at the edge of his world, or clouds way off in the distance. He's so close I could reach up and hug him goodnight like I used to, but of course I don't. Instead, I close my eyes and roll over. He might be standing right here over me, but I know the Dad who used to hug me really isn't here at all.

He sighs; then at last he walks around to the other side of the bed, stoops down, and carefully lifts up Sary to carry her back to her room.

CHAPTER 15

Partly because it's Saturday, but mostly because she's invited Billy to come for dinner, Lorrie sics chores on us so fast we don't have a chance to look for Tulip. Right after breakfast we clean the bathrooms, then I go to much out Heidi's stall while Lorrie keeps Sary cornered in the house folding laundry.

I'm almost finished in the barn—putting the pitchfork aside, picking up the broom—when I look out the door and see them walking side by side across the pasture. Lorrie's holding Sary by the hand and they're headed toward the cotton-woods.

It doesn't take me long to figure out they're going after Tulip. I bet Sary expects she'll be back before I know she's gone—that I'll never find out she's taking Lorrie with her to the creek.

Somewhere deep down I almost hope Wander will be there. If he is, if our secret gets out, maybe Lorrie really *can* fix things. I consider this idea for a moment, then change my mind.

Tossing the broom aside, I run out the door after them.

I keep out of sight and watch from the bushes. Sary has her back to me. She's standing beside Tulip's log, and I can hear her crying. Wander isn't around, thank goodness.

"She's gone, Lorrie. Tulip's gone."

"Are you sure this is where she was?" Lorrie asks.

"Yes. On this log. It's her place," Sary sobs.

I crouch in the brush while Lorrie helps Sary search. The last thing I want to do is get mixed up with Sary's crying, but I ought to do something. The way Lorrie's circling the clearing, leaning to peer beside every boulder and tree, pretty soon she's bound to discover Wander's tracks.

"I know I left her here." Sary points again to the old log where Tulip usually sits. "I know I did. When Wa—I mean, when *we* . . . found the bird's nest."

"Well, she's not here now. Maybe you took her home, and forgot. Are you sure she's not in your room? How about the kitchen?"

"No. She was right here." Sary plunks down on the log and sets into some serious crying.

Lorrie sits down too and tries to console her. "Now, don't look so forlorn," she says. "I'm sure Tulip'll turn up somewhere."

Lorrie stays with Sary until she stops crying. At last she says, "Tell me, where did you find that nest?"

"It was on the ground, over there." Sary points to the alder tree across the clearing. "Do you think Tulip will come back like the birds?"

"What birds?"

"The ones that go away for the winter. James told me they'll come back. But Tulip can't come back like them, can she?"

"No," Lorrie says, hugging Sary. "Somebody has to find her. And I'm sure you will."

Sary's beginning to calm down and goes chattering on. "How do the birds know to come back here? To this same place?"

"It's called instinct. Something inside that tells them this is where they belong."

"Like Daddy?" Sary asks.

"What do you mean?"

"Well, he leaves, but he always comes back home."

"Yes, Sary. But your dad comes home because he loves you."

As she says this, a breeze comes up, rustling the

brush where I'm hiding. Sary goes pale when she turns around and sees me.

"I didn't . . . ," she begins, then scowls and says, "What are you doing here?"

Lorrie slaps her knees. "Maybe he came to help us hunt for Tulip." She stands up, dusting off the back of her pants.

Sary gets up too and quickly crosses the clearing to join me, even though she knows full well I want to strangle her for bringing Lorrie to the creek.

"James," she says, innocently taking my hand, "come help me look for Tulip."

"I'll help you look at the house," I tell her, squeezing her hand hard and nearly dragging her out of the clearing.

"Don't, James," she says, pulling away from me as we head up the path. "It's okay. Wander wasn't there."

I stop to clap my hand over her mouth. "You want the whole danged valley to hear you? Keep quiet!"

Sary's standing in the path looking sad all over again when Lorrie joins us.

"You guys okay?" she says. "Sure are a couple of slowpokes today. Come on! I'll race you home!" She takes off running across the field and beats us to the house by a mile.

CHAPTER 16

Dad has come home and is waiting for us on the front porch.

"I want you both to stay close by today," he begins, taking the steps down to the walkway to meet us. "Wes Tiegland ambushed me down at Yolanda's this morning. He's all fired up about that stray dog. He's coming out here to go after it sometime this afternoon."

His words strike me like a slap in the face.

Sary doesn't move. We're so still anyone watching might think a funeral was happening right here in the yard. Neither of us says a word.

"Did you hear me, kids? Wes is coming. And he'll have his gun. I'm sorry now I ever told him about seeing that stray, but what's done is done.

And I don't want you out in the woods or any-place where he might mistake you for a dog."

I'm standing as dumb as one of those old cot-tonwood stumps, but inside I can feel my heart trying to trade places with my stomach.

How long has it been since Wander was just "that stray" to Sary and me? I look up at Dad and almost wish he could see inside me to that secret.

"What makes him think the dog's here?" My voice goes all husky and uneven.

Dad folds his arms across his chest. "He's searched everywhere else in the county for it al-ready. He's talked himself into believing that stray's murdering his sheep. Hunting it down is his way, and we're in no position to keep him from it."

"But what if the dog belongs to somebody?" Sary asks. "You told us that, Daddy. You told us he must belong to someone."

"It's been almost two weeks now, Sary. The dog's likely long gone. Or already dead. If Wes wants to go looking, it's fine with me. I don't want a dog running loose around here any more than he does. And it's his privilege, after all. He owns the land."

Abruptly Sary turns and runs down the path to the barn.

Dad shakes his head and walks by me, out to the driveway. The gate squeals on its hinge and I watch it swing back and forth until it finally settles on its latch with a hard metallic click.

I stand alone in the yard, helplessly letting Dad go on his way again. But how can I tell him the truth now? I wouldn't even know where to start.

The porch door opens behind me.

"Where's Sary?" Lorrie asks. "I thought she was coming in to look for Tulip." There's an unusually serious expression on her face as she comes down the steps to me.

"I guess she went to look for her in the barn," I say.

She sighs. "I tried to reach Billy, to tell him not to come until later, but he didn't answer. God, I hope he's not already on his way. If he shows up, I just know he'll get into a spat with Wes." She looks off expectantly toward the end of the driveway. "Oh, well. I suppose all we can do is wait and see what happens. Now go after your sister, James. Tell her it's time to come in."

I find Sary in the loft. She's opened the hay doors and is sitting with her knees up to her chin, staring out over the pasture. I sit down beside her.

I know she's expecting me to tell her that Wes's coming is no big deal. I suppose I *could* tell her Billy might show up to fix things, but there's no sense in giving her a hope like that.

"Can't you do something?" she says after a moment.

"It's too late." I pick up a piece of straw to chew on, partly to keep back how worried I feel, partly to keep back my anger. I know if I let my temper come up, I'll probably cry. "Wes Tiegland is already on his way."

"Tell Daddy, James," Sary pleads. "Just tell him. Tell him Wander was with us."

"What difference would that make? He wouldn't care."

"We can tell him we know Wander didn't kill those sheep."

"And how can we know that?" I ask.

"He was with us."

"Not when it rained. And not at night, he wasn't."

"Oh," she says. I realize she's struck for the first time by the possibility that Wander might very well have killed Mr. Tiegland's sheep.

"See what I mean?" I say. "It wouldn't do any good. We'd just get into trouble."

"Do you think Wander will come back? Do you think he'll wait at the creek for us?"

"Leave me alone, Sary. I don't want to talk about it anymore. There's nothing I can do."

"That's all you ever do, James."

"What's that?"

"Nothing," she replies. "*Nothing* is all you ever do."

CHAPTER 17

We're on our way back to the house when Wes Tiegland drives through the gate. His big old tires raise a splatter of mud as he pulls his truck up to the fence. Dad walks over and opens his door.

Wes gets out and stands by the truck. Dressed in his camouflage jacket and hunting cap, he looks ready to kill a whole herd of buffalo.

He's chewing on his lower lip, checking out Sary and me. Mr. Tiegland is the kind of man who hardly ever speaks to kids. If he does, it's usually roundabout, through somebody else, as in, "Hey, Dan. Kids are getting mighty grown up," or "What are you feeding those two, Lorrie?"

I catch him almost smiling at Sary, but then he

looks at Dad and says, "You'd better keep your youngsters at a distance."

"Want a cup of coffee before we head out?" Dad asks.

Apparently Wes isn't in the mood to be sociable. "No," he grumbles without offering so much as a "Thank you kindly." He shifts on his feet, a small ball of sunlight reflecting off his gun. "I'm anxious to get that devil in my sights."

"No sign of the dog up on your place?" Dad asks.

"No more than six dead sheep."

"Did you check with Aaron Navarro?"

"That idiot doesn't know the first thing about the predators around here. Fool thinks it's a mountain lion. But I've seen dogs run sheep just for the fun of it. A frenzy, you know."

"One dog?" Dad ventures. To anybody but Wes Tiegland he'd be making some sense—it's usually a pack of dogs that'll run stock, not just one, all alone.

"Who cares? One dog or twenty, I've still got six dead sheep up on my place. And talk's cheap. Let's get on with it."

"Where do you want to begin?"

"The creek's a fair place," Wes says. "There's water and shelter there."

It's the flash of movement in the woods behind Wes Tiegland that I notice before anything else, like the first day Wander came to us—he's a shadow almost, coming to the far end of the pasture to watch us from just beyond the cottonwood stumps. There's not much to tell it's a dog, but Sary reaches out and digs her fingers into my arm. She sees him too. I manage to smile at Wes.

He takes a step like he's about to turn toward the woods, so I plant myself directly in his way and ask, "What kind of gun is that?"

"It's a rifle," he answers, obviously annoyed.

"It's nice." I reach out to touch the barrel of the gun, trying to think what in the world I'm going to say next—anything to keep Wes from turning around. "You know . . . you know . . . I think we saw that dog again."

Wes grips his gun. "Saw him? Where?"

I'm not real sure what I'm doing. I just know I have to stall him until Wander has a chance to get away, or until Billy gets here—if he's coming at all. "Up on the hill," I say, turning to raise my hand in the opposite direction, to the ridge behind the house.

Dad looks confused. "When were you up there?"

"The day it rained," I reply, lying easy as syrup. "Lorrie said we couldn't go to the creek so we went up there to check for salamanders in the water tank."

"Oh." Dad nods, then looks at Sary. "Did *you* see the dog too?"

"Uh-huh. Like James said. Up there."

Wes steps toward us. "Why didn't you say so sooner?" He kneels down to Sary and grabs hold of her arm. He's squinting at her with his face up close to hers. Just watching him, I can almost smell the cigarette smoke on his breath and the salami he probably had for lunch.

"Why didn't you tell us?" Wes bellows. "I've lost two of my sheep since it rained."

"I—I don't know," Sary stammers. She's trying to pull away while she stares down at her shoes.

I'm praying, *Please, Billy . . . please, show up.*

Dad says, "Leave her be, Wes."

Wes lets go of her, stands up, and turns to me. "You telling the truth this time?"

"Yessir," I say. "We saw the dog. For sure."

"What was it doing?"

Sary's eyes are on me. "Just prowling," I say. "Looking for something to eat, I guess."

"Lamb chops." Wes zips the front of his jacket and tucks his gun under his arm. "You coming, Dan? I'm going to kill me a dog."

"Okay," Dad says. He shakes his head at us with his lips tight together. "We'll discuss this later. I want you two to stay right here."

Wes would be starting across the pasture already, but the rumble of Billy's truck rolling up from Route 5 stops him. I can see Billy at the gate now, and I glance hopefully at Sary.

When Billy drives in, he stops right in front of Wes. He cuts the engine, hops out of the truck, and slams the door.

"What are you doing here, Tiegland?" he asks. "Going after that imaginary bloodthirsty sheep-eating dog?" There's an anger coming up in Billy's blue eyes like I've never seen before.

Wes's jaw tightens; then he almost laughs. "If you had more than garbage to look after, Billy, maybe you'd appreciate what I do for a living."

"Oh, don't get me wrong, Tiegland. I appreciate every little bit of what you do. It's what you're *about* to do I'm not so keen on."

Fuming, Wes paces back and forth, his gun in his right hand. I can tell he's just itching to use it. "I don't have to explain anything to you," he says. "I've lost six sheep since last Monday—one of my prize ewes just two nights ago. You ought to know I'm not going to put up with that when I can take care of it with one shot from this." He shakes his gun at Billy.

Dad steps between them and grabs Wes's arm. "Take it easy. We're in this together. I don't want anything running around, dog or mountain lion, that's liable to go after Sary or James . . ."

I'm just starting to think we might be free and

116

clear, what with Dad speaking up and Billy here to help, when all of a sudden—and without a consideration for what she's doing—Sary leans way around Wes to look past him toward the woods and Wander.

Wes turns to follow her gaze. I'm praying his eyesight is as bad as his temper, but it isn't. He stops dead in his tracks. "I'll be whipped," he says, his voice like an icy wind. "Will you look at that?"

CHAPTER 18

Dad and Billy turn at the same time.

"What the . . . ?" Dad says.

Wes raises his gun. Billy moves swiftly to stop him.

"Let me by, you fool! That dog's got something in its mouth!" Wes is ready to take aim just as the front door slams and Lorrie comes running down the porch steps.

"Are you guys crazy? Put that gun down!" She charges up behind Wes and knocks his gun aside.

"Hell if I will!" He spits out of the corner of his mouth. "Lady, that dog's a killer! Check it out! It's got something in its—"

"I don't care. You're not going to shoot *anything* in front of these kids." She's so mad her face looks red enough to explode. "Haven't you got any sense at all?" She bends down and rings Sary and me with her arms.

Dad grabs Wes and swings him around. "She's right," he says.

"Let go, Christie!" Wes yells back as he breaks away from Dad. "I'm going to lose my shot!"

"For God's sake, put that gun down!" Lorrie screams.

Billy takes hold of the barrel of Wes's gun.

"James," Dad says to me, calm as anything, "take your sister to the house."

"He isn't a killer, Dad." I look up at him and let the words come. "He was with us."

Wes glares at me. "Don't lie, kid."

"He's not," Sary says. "He's our dog."

"You raise *two* liars, Christie?" Wes shouts, pulling his gun away from Billy.

"For your information, *Mr.* Tiegland," Dad says in a stony voice, "my children are not liars."

Wes laughs. "Well, for *your* information, *Mr.* Christie, they're lying now."

"That's enough," Lorrie says.

"You can bet it's enough!" Wes answers. "If I don't get that animal, I'll be sending you the bill for the six sheep I've lost. You know, Christie, it's clear these kids of yours need a mother."

Wes Tiegland's words turn Dad's eyes so black and furious, for a moment he looks like another person, crazed almost. But just as quickly, his look turns sad and lost, and it seems he might just walk away and leave us all standing here in the yard.

Clearing his throat, Dad says, "I want you off our place, Tiegland. And I want you kids inside. Sary? Where are you going? Sary!"

Her feet must be deciding for her, that's all I can say. She sure isn't thinking. One second she's right here listening to the arguing, the next she's on her way across the pasture to Wander.

"Call that girl back!" Wes hollers. "Where does she think she's going? She'll spook that animal and I'll never get a shot at him!"

But Wander doesn't spook. He doesn't turn tail and run off. When he sees Sary coming, he gallops to the fence, takes it in a flying leap, and heads straight for her.

Dad's yelling, "Stop, Sary! Don't move!"

I grab his arm. "She'll be okay. He won't hurt her."

Wes lifts his gun and aims. "Hell if he won't!" he says.

"We know him!" I'm screaming. "He's our dog!"

"No he's not, kid. It's that stray. And your sister's about to get herself . . ." Wes moves forward. Dad reaches out and takes hold of his jacket.

"Let go of me, Christie!"

"That's my kid out there and you're not—"

With a sudden jerk, Wes pulls away and raises his gun again.

Both Billy and Dad come down on him then, nearly knocking Wes to the ground.

I begin to run.

It's not any distance at all. I've crossed this space almost every day without thinking about it—more times than I can count. But now it seems like there are a hundred miles spread between Sary and me.

Wander's reached Sary and he jumps up to greet her, just as the gun goes off.

CHAPTER 19

I know I heard a shot, but now the whole world's slowing down, sliding past me, like water pouring with no sound. I'm spinning—watching Wander drop what's in his mouth, watching Dad and Lorrie run toward me across the field—spinning—watching Wander fly back over the fence, then disappear—spinning, spinning—until I finally see Sary. She wheels around slowly—stands still in the middle of the field, facing me. Before I can get to her, she crumples to the ground in a little heap.

"Call somebody!" Lorrie's screaming as she and Billy and Dad run past me. "Wes! Get the doctor out here! Her number's by the phone!"

Wes Tiegland runs up and stands dumbfounded

beside me, his gun still in his hand. "I didn't mean to. It was an accident—"

"Shut up and call her, Wes!" Lorrie screams. "Damn you! Call Isabelle Gamboni! Call her, now!"

Wes drops his gun and stumbles away from me, half walking, half running across the driveway, through the gate, and into the house.

I'm so scared Sary's going to die that I can't do anything but stand frozen as Dad runs back toward the house. Sary trembling in his arms, her face pure white. A steady stream of blood is traveling down her arm. It leaves a trail of droplets in the dirt.

Wes comes running out onto the porch. "Dr. Gamboni's on her way. Is the kid okay? Is she going to be all right?"

Dad pushes by him without a word.

They've put my sister on the kitchen table. Dad's torn off Sary's shirt, and Lorrie's wrapped a twisted dishtowel above the bleeding part of her arm. I stand out of the way by the door, silent and shaking. Then Dad looks up at me.

"Take him out of here," he says to Billy.

Billy puts his hand on my shoulder and guides me out the door just as Isabelle arrives.

She slams her car door and runs up to the porch. "What's going on?"

"It's Sary," I manage to say. "She's in the kitchen. On the table. She's shot."

"Go on in," Billy says. "They're waiting for you."

Isabelle pauses beside me long enough to squeeze my hand; then she disappears inside the house.

Billy sits down beside me on the step.

"She'll be fine, James."

"Dad said we aren't liars, but we are." I choke back tears.

"I know," Billy said. "You lied to all of us."

"We lied and now Sary's going to die."

"No, no," Billy says. "She isn't going to die. The bullet only nicked her arm. Lorrie's slowed the bleeding and Isabelle's here now. Sary will be all right."

Yes. Isabelle's here now. Everything *has* to be all right.

"I should have done it different," I say. "I should have told Dad that we wanted to keep him. Sary wanted me to; I just didn't know how. I was afraid we'd be told no. I was afraid that telling would do him harm."

Billy takes hold of my hands, turning me so I have to look into his eyes. "You spoke up. That's what's really important."

"But if I'd done it sooner. If I'd done it different . . ."

"Don't bother fretting over what's already past, James. Just remember to do it differently next time."

Billy stays with me through the whole long wait while Isabelle's in the house with Sary. Wes paces up and down the length of the fence without speaking to us, his mind far off—his thoughts of killing gone for now.

I think about Wander, and about Sary lying there bleeding in the kitchen, hurt so bad she didn't even cry. And I think about Dad, sad and worried over Sary, with Isabelle beside him. Isabelle. Right here in this house, with us, after so long.

At last the door opens.

"She'll mend," Isabelle says, smiling at me in a reassuring way as she and Lorrie come out onto the porch. "I've wrapped her up and given her an injection. She'll sleep for a while, then she'll be up and around, no problem." She turns to Lorrie. "Gunshot, though. I'll have to make a report." She glances across the yard at Wes. "He the one?"

Lorrie nods.

"Is—Is she okay?" Wes stammers, charging up to the gate but not coming through. "Is the little girl okay? I didn't mean to hit her. It was that dog. You know, it's not my fault; they should have just let me shoot it."

Billy sighs in disgust and stands up. "I can't listen to this," he says. "I'm going for a walk." Without another word, he heads down the driveway and out into the pasture.

Isabelle signals to Wes. She meets him outside the fence. "I need to speak to you," she says. They turn so I can't hear, but I know she's asking him a lot of questions. It takes some time, but when she finishes, she comes back to the porch where I'm waiting.

"I'm sorry, James, but I've got to go. The office is always full on Saturdays. I'll be back to check on Sary tomorrow. You guys still like ice cream, don't you?"

"Yes. Sary likes chocolate best."

"I remember." Isabelle moves a wisp of hair off my face. She smiles and touches my cheek, her touch familiar and warm. "I've missed you guys, you know." She's about to go, but then she takes me quickly into her arms, hugging me hard. "Tell your dad I'll be here around ten."

She leaves, hurrying down the walkway and through the gate without so much as a nod to Wes. She swings open her car door, gets in, waves good-bye once more, then drives away.

Shaken but still angry, Wes comes over and

leans against the fence. "I'm sorry about your sister," he says. "But you shouldn't have lied like that—"

"It's time for you to go, Wes," Lorrie says. "Leave James alone. Haven't you done enough harm for one day?"

"This wouldn't have happened if he'd told the truth in the first place. He shouldn't have pretended he knew that dog."

Billy's walking up the driveway. He stops behind Wes. "He didn't," he says. "James told you the truth about that."

"And how do *you* know?"

Billy ignores him and walks up to me on the porch. He stops in front of me, takes his hands from behind his back, and shows me what he's holding.

"She belongs to Sary, doesn't she?"

I nod as he lays Tulip gently on my lap. "It's Tulip-Virginia," I say. "It's Sary's doll."

Billy swings around to face Wes. "*This,* Mr. Tiegland, is what that dog had in his mouth. Now go home. It's over. Go home now or I'll call the sheriff like I should have done an hour ago."

We don't stay to watch Wes leave. Lorrie takes Billy by the hand and they go inside to clean up the kitchen, holding the door open for me to follow.

"You coming, James?" Lorrie asks.

"Yeah," I say, letting the screen back easy on its hinge.

I climb the stairs as quietly as I can when I go up to Sary's room, realizing I'm holding Tulip in my arms as tenderly as if I were holding a real baby and not just my sister's beat-up old rag doll.

CHAPTER 20

A pale, dusty glow filters through the curtain, barely lighting Sary's room but casting a ribbon of hazy yellow across the bed, where Dad's sitting, stroking her hair.

When I pause in the doorway, he looks up. "What's that?" he asks, standing slowly so as not to jostle Sary.

I walk over to the bed, and she smiles up at me sleepily when I lay Tulip on the quilt beside her.

Dad reaches out and takes my hand. "You all right, James?"

"Sure, Dad. Is she going to be okay?"

"Yes," he says, pulling me close to him. His voice is hardly more than a whisper. "Sary was a brave girl today. Brave, just like her mother."

Maybe it's the gloomy light in this room that makes me feel like crying. Or maybe it's Dad's big hand coming up to touch the back of my head.

I can't help but stay here and let him hold me. There's something wonderful about leaning against his chest, listening to him breathe. I can hear his heartbeat too, faint but fast, and behind it, a soft, sweet humming sound—a sound I know from long ago, a sound so familiar it feels like it's coming from inside me too.

I can't hold my tears. They come at last, dampening Dad's shirt as he hums softly and rocks me back and forth.

"She'll be fine," he says after a moment, thinking I'm crying over Sary. "She'll be fine."

I feel a terrible hurt starting to rise up inside me. He ought to know different. He ought to understand it's him holding me like this that's making me cry. Suddenly I'm embarrassed. Now all I know is I can't keep standing here in his arms all night aching inside and weeping like a baby.

"I'd better go down and help Lorrie in the kitchen," I say, pulling away from him and wiping my eyes. "She needs me to set the table."

Dad stays upstairs with Sary while I eat dinner in the kitchen with Lorrie and Billy. They seem so wrapped up in each other they hardly notice me,

and the meal's over by the time I realize I probably should have left them alone.

Dad finally comes down while we're doing the
dishes.

"Did she eat anything?" Lorrie asks.

"A little soup," Dad answers wearily. "She's
sleeping now."

"The best thing for her," Billy says.

"Yes. I guess it is," says Dad.

I keep back by the refrigerator, wanting him to
look at me, or to come over and speak to me,
maybe offer to help me dry the dishes—wanting
him to do *something*, since we seemed so close upstairs.

But I can feel him moving away, and as he walks
past me, that dark, empty quiet comes flooding
up around us.

I can't believe it. Just like any night, he's taking
his jacket off the back of his chair.

"You going out?" Lorrie asks. She doesn't even
bother to look around as Dad starts for the door.

But he stops before he gets there, just for a second, and turns to Lorrie as he puts on his jacket.
"There's something I have to do."

"Something I have to do." "Someone I need to
see." Why does he even bother to give her an
explanation?

He's reaching for the doorknob now, opening
the door, going through, starting to close it be-

hind him. Even with Sary so hurt upstairs, and me right here in front of him, he still can't stand to stay?

I don't know—maybe it's this hurt ready to burst inside me that's making me go after him. Suddenly my feet are taking me across the room, without me telling them, like Sary's feet must have taken her across the field this afternoon. There are words in my throat, too heavy to stay. Rushing to the door, I swing it wide.

"Dad!" I cry out, running down the steps, down the walkway. I grab hold of his hand. "Dad, wait!"

I'm clutching his hand so hard. Maybe that's why he's staring at me with such a surprised look on his face—as if he's just recognized who I am.

"Dad, don't go, okay?"

His eyes turn gentle as he looks down at me— almost smiling, the way they used to, and full of love. He squeezes my hand. "I won't, James," he says. "I won't. But there's something I have to do. Wait here. It's starting to rain."

In the misty half-light of evening I watch Dad walk out the front gate, down the driveway, and into the pasture.

Lorrie and Billy have come out onto the porch. "What's he doing?" Lorrie asks, worry coming up in her voice as Dad crosses the field toward the cottonwoods. I don't answer, though suddenly I think I know.

It's like music when my father whistles, the same long, true note I taught Sary. And my tears come again as I watch him standing alone by the cottonwood stumps in the rain, whistling over . . . and over . . . and over.

When Wander comes to the fence he's a little bit shy, hesitating the way he did the first day with Sary and me. Then Dad kneels, stretches out his hand, and whistles again, this time low and coaxing. Wander's tail flutters; then he jumps the fence and runs to him.

ABOUT THE AUTHOR

Susan Hart Lindquist has always lived in California. She received a bachelor's degree from the University of California, Santa Barbara. A writing instructor, a poet, and the author of a previous novel, *Walking the Rim,* she is currently at work on a third children's novel. She lives in Walnut Creek with her husband, Paul, and their children, Charlie, Madeline, and Sam.